Blonde Hair, Blue Eyes

Also by Karin Slaughter

Blonde Hair, Blue Eyes

A SHORT STORY

KARIN SLAUGHTER

WITNESS
IMPULSE

An Imprint of HarperCollinsPublishers

Excerpt from *Pretty Girls* copyright © 2015 by Karin Slaughter.

EPub Edition AUGUST 2015 ISBN: 9780062442819
Print Edition ISBN: 9780062442871

10 9 8 7

Monday, March 4, 1991
7:26 a.m.—North Lumpkin Street, Athens, Georgia

The morning mist laced through the downtown streets, spiderwebbing tiny, intricate patterns onto the sleeping bags lining the sidewalk outside the Georgia Theater. The doors wouldn't open for at least another twelve hours, but the Phish devotees were determined to have front row seats. Two heavyset young men filled plastic lawn chairs by the chained front door. At their feet were beer cans, cigarette butts, and an empty sandwich bag that had likely contained a large amount of weed.

Their eyes followed Julia Carroll as she walked down the street. She could feel their collective gaze clinging to her body as closely as the mist. She kept her head trained forward, her back straight, but then she wondered if she looked cold, haughty, and then she wondered with some annoyance why it mattered how she looked to these boys who were complete strangers.

She never used to be this paranoid.

Athens was a college town, anchored by the University of Georgia, which took up almost eight hundred acres of prime real estate and employed in some capacity over half of the county. Julia had grown up here. She was a student in the journalism program, a reporter for the campus newspaper. Her father was a professor at the college of veterinary sciences. At nineteen years old, she knew that alcohol and circumstance could turn nice-looking boys into the kind of people you didn't want to run into at seven-thirty on a Monday morning.

Or maybe she was being silly. Maybe this was like the time she was walking late at night in front of Old College and she heard footsteps behind her and saw a looming, speeding shadow and her heart flipped and she wanted to run but then the scary man had called out her name and it was only Ezekiel Mann from biology class.

He had talked to her about his brother's new car, then started quoting Monty Python lines, and Julia had picked up her pace so quickly that they were both jogging by the time they reached her dorm. Ezekiel had pressed his hand against the closed glass door as she'd signed herself into the building.

"I'll call you!" he'd practically yelled.

She had smiled at him and thought, *Oh, God, please don't make me hurt your feelings,* as she'd made her way toward the stairs.

Julia was beautiful. She had known this since she was a child, but rather than embrace the gift, she had always seen it as a burden. People made assumptions about beautiful girls. They were the icy, backstabby bitches who always got their comeuppance in John Hughes movies. They were the trophies that no boy in school dared to claim. Everyone took her shyness for aloofness. Her mild anxiety for disapproval. That these assumptions had left her a near-friendless virgin at the ripe age of nineteen went unremarked upon by everyone but her two younger sisters.

College was supposed to be different. Sure, her dorm was less than a quarter mile from her family home, but this was Julia's chance to reinvent herself, to be the person she had always wanted to be: strong, confident, happy, content (not a virgin). She squelched her natural propensity to sit reading in her room while the world passed outside her door. She joined the tennis club, the track club, and the wildlife club. She didn't choose cliques. She spoke to everyone. She smiled at strangers. She went on dates with boys who were sweet if not terribly interesting, and whose desperate kisses reminded her of a lamprey eel burrowing its tongue into the side of a lake trout.

But then Beatrice Oliver happened.

Julia had followed the girl's story on the telex at the *Red & Black*, UGA's campus newspaper. Nineteen years old, the same as Julia. Blonde hair and blue eyes, the same as Julia. College student, the same as Julia.

Beautiful.

Five weeks ago, Beatrice Oliver had left her parents' house around ten o'clock in the evening. She was on foot, walking to the store to get some ice cream for her father, who was suffering from a toothache. Julia wasn't sure why that part of the story stuck out to her. It seemed suspect—why would you want something cold on an aching tooth?—but that was what both parents had told the police, so that detail was in the story.

And the story was on the telex because Beatrice Oliver had never come home.

Julia was obsessed with the girl's disappearance. She told herself it was because she wanted to cover the story for the *Red & Black*, but the truth was that it scared her to death to know that someone—not just someone, but a girl her own age—could walk out the door and never come back again. Julia wanted to know the details. She wanted to talk to the girl's parents. She wanted to interview Beatrice Oliver's friends or a cousin or a neighbor or a coworker or a boyfriend or another boyfriend or anyone who might offer an alternate explanation other than that a nineteen year-old girl with her entire life ahead of her had just vanished into thin air.

"We are looking at a likely abduction," the detective in the first story had been quoted as saying. All of Beatrice's personal belongings were accounted for, including her purse, the cash she kept in her sock drawer, and her car, which was still parked in the family's driveway.

The most chilling statement came from Beatrice Oliver's mother: "The only reason my daughter has not come home is because someone is keeping her."

Keeping her.

Julia shuddered at the thought of being kept—from her family, from her life, from her freedom. In her childhood books, the bogeyman was always scraggly and dark and looming, a wolf in sheep's clothing, but clearly (if you looked carefully) still a wolf. She knew that real life wasn't like those fairy tales. You couldn't easily spot the telltale mustache and goatee that indicated the wolf was a Bad Man.

Whoever had Beatrice Oliver could be a friend or a coworker or a neighbor or a boyfriend or another boyfriend—all of the people that Julia wanted to interview face-to-face. Alone. With just a pad and pen. Talking to a man who might at that very moment be keeping Beatrice Oliver somewhere awful.

Julia put her hand to her stomach to calm the churning. She checked behind her, left and right, her eyeballs feeling jittery in her head.

She tried to logic down some of her anxiety. It was possible she was winding herself up for no reason. The Beatrice Oliver interviews might not even happen. Before Julia spoke to anyone, she would need to get the story assignment okayed, because a news journalist could legitimately ask questions but a features writer (Julia's section) was just being nosy. Her biggest obstacle would be Greg Gianakos, the student editor in chief who thought he was the next Walter Cronkite and reminded Julia of what her father said about beagles: They love to hear the sound of their own voices.

If she could get Greg on board, then Lionel Vance, Greg's minion, would follow (even though he was sulking because she'd turned him down for a date). The final hurdle would be Mr. Hannah, the faculty advisor, who was very nice, but preferred story pitch meetings to play out like a Mexican cliff diving match on the *Wide World of Sports*.

Julia silently practiced the pitch as she turned down the next empty street.

Beatrice Oliver, a nineteen-year-old girl who lives with her parents. . .

No, they would be making snoring noises before she finished the sentence.

A missing girl!

No. Lots of girls went missing. They usually showed up a few days later.

A young girl was walking to the store late at night when suddenly. . .

Julia spun around.

She'd heard a noise behind her. A scraping sound, like shoes scuffing the street. She scanned the area again, eyes picking out broken pieces of glass and old beer bottles and discarded newspapers, but there was nothing. At least nothing that she should be worried about.

Slowly, carefully, she resumed her walk, still checking doorways and alleys, and crossing the street so she wouldn't have to pass by a massive mound of trash.

Paranoid.

Reporters were supposed to look at events with a cold eye toward the facts, but since reading about Beatrice Oliver, Julia's dreams had been filled with details that came not from fact, but from her own wild imagination. Beatrice was walking down the street. The night was dark. The moon was obscured. There was a chill in the air. She saw the glow of a lit cigarette, heard the soft patter of shoes on asphalt, and then tasted a nicotine-stained hand clamping over her mouth, felt a razor-sharp knife at her throat, smelled the acidic breath of a menacing stranger as he dragged her toward his car and locked her in the trunk, then drove her somewhere dark and dank where he could keep her.

If Julia's mother were not a librarian, she would probably blame Julia's dark imaginings on the books she was reading. *The Stranger Beside Me. Helter Skelter. The Silence of the Lambs. The Witching Hour.* But her mother *was* a librarian, so she would probably shrug and tell her eldest daughter to not read stories that scared her.

Or did being scared of these things, putting voice to her terrible fears, immunize Julia from danger?

She wiped sweat from her brow. Her heart was pounding so hard that she could feel the tickling of her T-shirt against her skin. She reached into her purse. Her Walkman was nestled inside the yellow scarf she had promised her sister she'd drop by the house. Her finger rested on the play button, but she didn't press it. She just wanted to feel the cassette tape inside, to summon the scrawled handwriting of the boy who had made it for her.

Robin Clark.

Julia had met him two months ago. There had been notes passed back and forth, phone calls, pages, a few group dates where their eyes lingered and their hands touched, and then they'd finally been alone and he had kissed her so long and so well that the top of her head nearly exploded. She had brought him home once, not to meet her parents but to pick up her laundry. Her youngest sister had laughed about Robin being a girl's name until Julia had punched her in the arm and made her stop. (For once, the little brat hadn't tattled.)

The mix tape had songs that Robin thought Julia would like, not songs he wanted her to like. So instead of

Styx and Chicago and Metallica, there were Belinda Carlisle and Wilson Phillips and a little Beatles and James Taylor and lots of Madonna, because Robin thought that Madonna was just as awesome as Julia did.

The tape was the first time in her life that a boy had seen her for who she was rather than who he wanted her to be. Julia had spent so many years pretending to like drum solos and screechy guitars and bootlegged copies of artists who had tragically died before they could prove to the world (and not just the boy who'd made the mix tape) how cool they were.

Robin didn't want Julia to pretend. He wanted her to be herself, and her women's studies professor would've probably had a heart attack to learn that Julia, finally, wanted to be herself—but only because she'd found a boy who wanted that, too.

"Robin," Julia whispered into the cool morning air, because she loved the way his name felt in her mouth. "Robin."

He was twenty-two years old, rangy and tall, with ropy biceps from lifting heavy trays of bread at his father's bakery. He had shaggy brown-almost-black Jon Bon Jovi hair and blue eyes like a husky dog and when he looked at Julia, she felt a deep stirring in a place that she didn't quite have a name for.

There had been a few boys before Robin. They were usually older like he was (though never as mature), the kind of guys who weren't overly intimidated by the way Julia looked because they had cars and money in their pockets. Her father had warned Julia that these boys only wanted one thing. What he didn't understand was that Julia wanted that one thing, too.

Second base. That was as far as she'd ever gotten, unless there was a position for pleasant rubbing (short stop?) Brent Lockwood had been sixteen (almost seventeen) to Julia's fifteen (closer to fourteen). He had asked her father for permission to take her out, and her father had told him to get a haircut, get a job, and get back to him.

That Brent would return a few days later with a buzz cut and an apron from McDonald's was news that had surprised her father, tickled her mother, and sent her sisters into howls of laughter. Julia had been outraged. Brent's hair had been the best part of him. Henceforth, the odor of grilled meat dug into his cropped scalp like teeth. Julia was a vegetarian. Being around Brent was a wretchedly unfunny variation on Pavlov's experiment.

And still, she had tried (in the back of his car; on the living room couch), because Brent was handsome and everyone knew he'd been with a lot of girls and this was Julia's chance to get it over with. She wanted so desperately to be the sophisticated girl everyone thought she was: the one who knew her way around a boy, the one who had experience, the jaded, beautiful girl who could wrap a man around her little finger.

But Brent had been in love with her, and he'd wanted to be gentle, and to go slow, which—combined with the greasy French-fryness of his skin—was excruciatingly boring.

Robin Clark was not boring on any level. He smelled really nice, like pine with a not unpleasing bready undertone from the bakery. His skin was beautifully tan from hiking and biking all year round. He looked into Julia's eyes when she talked to him. He didn't try to solve her problems; he just listened. He laughed at her jokes, even the bad ones (especially the bad ones). He could be dreamy, too. He wanted to be an artist. He already *was* an artist (the bakery job was temporary). Julia had seen some of his work. The gentle slope of a deer's neck as it dipped its mouth toward a mountain spring. The crazy reds and oranges of a sunrise. His hand gently wrapped around the curve of Julia's hip.

He had sketched this image on a napkin before making a move. He'd shown it to Julia over a cup of tea in the student center and told her that the drawing showed what he wanted to do. Her knees shook when it was time to stand. Her palms were sweaty. She had been so giddy with anticipation that by the time he actually put his hand at her waist, his fingers felt electrified against her skin.

"I'm going to kiss you," he had whispered into her ear right before he did.

Julia pulled her hand away from the Walkman. The homeless shelter van where she volunteered was parked at the intersection of Hull and Washington, an area of town that for unknown reasons was called Hot Corner. People were already lined up for breakfast. There were at least thirty of them, mostly men, a few women. They shuffled along in line, heads down, hands in their pockets. Everything about them said that they hated taking charity, but they needed charity, and so they were resigned to standing in line at the crack of dawn so they could have at least one hot meal.

"Good morning," Candice Bender called. She was handing out tinfoil containers with scrambled eggs, bacon, grits, and toast. The large coffee urn at the mouth of the open van doors was self-serve.

"Sorry I'm late." Julia wasn't late, but she had the nervous habit of starting conversations with some kind of apology. She grabbed a stack of blankets from the van and took in the line of people. Someone was missing. "Where's Mona No-Name?"

Candice shrugged.

Julia stepped back to get a closer look at the line. Her fear rose exponentially as she checked each face.

"Don't see her?" Candice asked.

Julia shook her head. She had done this long enough to know that people moved on, but she could not hold back the sinister thoughts that came seeping in.

Mona was young, just a few months older than Julia. Compared to the others, she took better care of herself, bathed more, wore nicer clothes, because she wasn't wasting all of her money on drugs. She'd been thrown out of the foster system on her eighteenth birthday and ended up doing the things some girls had to do in order to survive. When Julia had asked for her last name, Mona had defiantly declared, "Bitch, I ain't got no name."

"Mona No-Name it is," Julia had said, because she had been in a bad mood and slightly hung over from an impromptu evening of picklebacks and cheese crackers. (To her great shame, the moniker had stuck.)

"Mo-No wasn't here last night," one of the women said as she took a clean blanket.

Julia asked, "When did you see her last?"

"How the hell would I know?"

They didn't look out for each other, the women. There was competition. There was gossip. What passed for a social scene reminded Julia of high school because they created the same roles: the whore, the teacher's pet, the good girl, the bitch, the nerd. Mona was the bitch because she was pretty—she still had all of her teeth, she wore makeup, she didn't look homeless. Delilah was the whore because she was older and more experienced. And also because she really was a whore.

Currently, there was a total of eight women in the group, and unlike with Beatrice Oliver, who had been abducted on a trip to get ice cream for her father, Julia knew that the dark things her mind conjured about the homeless women's lives were more than likely correct. Prostitution. Drugs. Hunger. Sickness. Fear. Loneliness, because most homeless people, Julia had discovered, were incredibly, achingly, heartbreakingly lonely.

"I seen Mona go into the woods," Delilah said. "Say about ten, eleven last night, just before the rain come."

Julia nodded to let her know she'd heard.

Delilah was scary because she was unpredictable; given to screaming, crying, humming incessantly, or laughing so loudly that your ears rang like a bell. She was an addict, and had been on the streets for longer than Julia had been volunteering at the shelter. Delilah kept pictures of her grown children in her pocket and carried a kit of syringes she used only on herself. In the last four years, Julia had graduated high school, gotten into college, finished her freshman year with honors, and was promoted to editor of the features section at the *Red & Black*.

In that same time, Delilah had been rolled repeatedly, which was what the homeless people called being robbed. She had lost all of her front teeth in a fight, patches of her hair were falling out from lack of nutrition, and weird purpley brown lesions had leeched up from her skin.

AIDS, Julia thought, though no one said the word aloud because AIDS was a death sentence.

"There's a group of people living in the woods," Candice told Julia. "I went out there yesterday to see if they needed help, but apparently they're living outdoors because they think it's fun, not out of any dire circumstance."

Julia handed a blanket to a man wearing army fatigues. His black ball cap said "Vietnam MIA Never Forget." She asked Candice, "Choosing? Like, camping?" Robin was camping with his family this week. Julia hadn't been invited, but that was only because it would be weird to go on a sleepover date with his entire family. "Mona doesn't strike me as the camping type."

"The sheriff is calling them a cult." Candice gave an exaggerated frown. Like Julia's mother, she was a former hippie with a healthy skepticism of authority. "They're all around your age, maybe a little older. If you ask me, I'd say it's more like a commune. They dress alike. They talk alike. They act alike. It's a regular *Patty Duke Show*."

Julia suppressed a shudder. More like the Charles Manson Show. "Why would Mona go off with them?"

"Why wouldn't she?" Candice had finished handing out meals and turned to the blankets. "Their plan, inasmuch as there is one, is to walk the Appalachian Trail to Mount Katahdin, they said, but it sounds more like an excuse to stop bathing and screw like rabbits."

"I'm in!" Vietnam bellowed.

Julia asked Candice, "Where are they camping?"

"Just past the Wishing Rock."

So, nowhere near where Robin and his family were camping this week.

"What do you think of that?" Candice asked. She was a retired schoolteacher, still desperate for a young mind to mold. "Leaving home, abandoning all of your worldly possessions, living off the land. Could you see yourself doing that?"

Julia shrugged, though she could more easily see herself walking on the moon. "They're free spirits, right? That's kind of romantic."

Candice smiled. This was obviously the right answer.

Julia grabbed a trash bag out of the box. She went about collecting the empty tins and coffee cups. She had no idea why it didn't bother her to clean up after these people when retrieving so much as a dirty sock that one of her lazy younger sisters had left on the stairs sent her into fits of rage.

She had started volunteering at the shelter shortly after her fifteenth birthday. It was summer. She was bored. There weren't any books she wanted to read. Her sisters were driving her crazy. She was sick of babysitting. She was sick of being in charge. She was sick of waiting to be an adult.

"Let's see if you've got what it takes to do this," her father had told her in the car on the way to the shelter.

"What?" Julia had snapped, because she didn't know what "this" was, that her father was taking her to the bad side of town where she would be expected to wait on smelly, crazy homeless people.

The shelter was meant to be a Life Lesson, like the time her parents made them all choose one gift from Christmas to donate to the children's home and it couldn't be socks or underwear. Julia hated Life Lessons. She hated being forced to do things. She hated being tricked into getting in the car with her dad, who'd told her they were going to check on a new litter of puppies. She was stubborn (like her mother, her father said) and she was contrary (like her father, her mother said) and she was opinionated (like her parents, her grandmother said) and she was bossy (like her grandmother, her sisters said), and those were the only reasons she had stuck it out at the shelter those first few months.

I'll show him I can do this, Julia had silently seethed against her father, throwing herself into cooking and cleaning and doing laundry in a way that filled her mother with so much wryness that her lips were locked into a permanent zigzag.

"Julia washed dishes?" Her mother's voice trilled like the bell on a bike. "Julia Carroll, the older girl who lives here in this house?"

What kept Julia going back to the shelter was hard to explain. She didn't particularly enjoy laundering filthy clothes or scrubbing toilets. And yet, two or three times a week, she forced herself out of bed at seven in the morning and walked to skid row or to the shelter on Prince Avenue so that she could hand out food and blankets or clean up after drug addicts, mental cases, and other lost souls.

Because of how she looked, people tended to want Julia.

The people she served through the shelter *needed* her.

Candace asked, "Mind finishing up for me, kiddo? I have a meeting with the mayor."

"Of course." Julia tossed the trash bag into the van. She grabbed some pens and a stack of papers from the front seat—forms that needed to be filled out, requests for disability and veterans' benefits and Medicaid.

For the next few hours, Julia did paperwork and made phone calls to state agencies on the stinky pay phone and talked to some of the group about what they were going to do with their lives. Many of Julia's friends scoffed at her volunteer work (they thought homeless people were lazy), but what they did not understand was that people generally ended up living on the streets not through some deep character flaw but through a cascading series of seemingly minor bad choices—pissing off the wrong cop, hanging out with the wrong people, missing school or work or a parole meeting because they had been too exhausted to remember to set their alarm clock.

Julia wasn't a psychiatrist, but many of them clearly

had some underlying mental health issue, whether it was mild paranoia, depression, or full-blown delusions.

"*Reagan*," her mother had said when Julia had first brought this phenomenon to her attention. "What did he think would happen when he cut federal aid to mental hospitals? They're all either living on the streets or in prisons."

Beatrice Oliver. The girl who went to get ice cream and was never seen again. She had been treated for depression, which was an actual mental illness. Julia had read as much on the telex. The Associated Press had sent a reporter to talk to the parents while they searched for their daughter (looking for her body, but no one said it) and the mother had admitted that Beatrice had once been treated for depression.

Julia had seen a psychiatrist her freshman year of college. She hadn't told anyone because it was embarrassing to admit that living away from her family wasn't as easy as she'd thought it would be. Toward the end of the session, the shrink had actually yawned, which had helped Julia more than his generic advice (join a group/try a new activity/get a new hairstyle/smile more), because it showed her that her problems were mundane, that the kids around campus who seemed to have all of their shit together were probably suffering from the same boring anxieties, too.

But it also made her wonder. If Julia went missing one day, or God forbid she was taken, would a reporter find out that she had talked to a shrink? And would talking to a shrink signify some kind of mental illness?

"She was took!" Delilah's harsh voice jolted Julia out of her thoughts. "Mark my words, sister woman."

Julia looked up from the letter she was writing to Delilah's daughter. The girl never wrote back, which seemed to disappoint Julia more than Delilah.

"She was took," Delilah repeated. "Mona No-Name. She was took by a man."

"Oh," was all Julia could think to say.

"Not like that," Delilah said. "He took her like—" Delilah grunted, circling her arms in a grabby, menacing hug.

Julia pulled in her own arms as if the man was grabbing her.

"She's walking down the street," Delilah said. "She gets past that old-timey car, and this black van pulls up and the door slides open, and this man, big man, white dude, he reaches out and—" She made the grabbing gesture again.

Julia rubbed her arms to soothe the chills. She saw the black van, the door sliding open, the blur of a clean-cut, all-American boy emerging from the pitch darkness. His arms were out. His fingers turned into claws. His mouth contorted into a snarl that showed razor-sharp teeth.

"Lissen'a me, girl." Delilah's voice was a menacing growl. "She was snatched. Any one'a us could get snatched. Any one'a you."

Julia put down her pen. She stared into Delilah's rheumy yellow eyes. Heroin. That's what the needles in Delilah's kit were for. Kaposi's sarcoma. That's what the skin lesions were from. Julia had written several articles about HIV and AIDS for the *Red & Black*. She knew that the rare cancer could spread to the organs, causing lesions on the brain. Delilah wasn't lucid in the best of times. Was she relaying some sort of vision, or fever dream? It didn't seem possible that someone could just be snatched off the street in the middle of downtown Athens.

Then again, it didn't seem possible a girl could be snatched walking from her parents' house to get ice cream for her dad.

Not just snatched.

Kept.

Still, Julia gently reminded Delilah, "Before, you said that you saw Mona go into the woods."

"The van had dirt caked around the tires. Grass and shit. Bet my right tit he took her into the woods." She leaned closer. Her breath reeked of rot and cigarettes. "Men do things to girls, darlin'. They get some time with 'em, they do things you don't wanna know about."

Julia felt every single hair on the back of her neck zing to attention.

"Ha!" Delilah laughed, because that's what she always did when she got a rise out of somebody. "Ha!" She grabbed her belly. No sound came from her mouth, but her head tilted back in an approximation of hilarity. Her empty gums glistened in the creeping sunlight.

Julia rubbed the back of her neck, soothing down the hairs.

Beatrice Oliver. Mona No-Name. They lived within twenty miles of each other. They were both pretty. They were both blonde. They were roughly the same age. They had both been walking down the street one night. Had they both been seen by an evil man who decided to take them?

The same evil man? Two different evil men? Were those men now both at home with their families? Were they each separately making breakfasts for their kids, or shaving their faces, or kissing their wives good-bye, all the while smiling to themselves as they considered what they would do later on to the girls they had taken?

"Hey." Delilah poked Julia's arm. "You gonna finish that? I got places to go."

Julia picked up the pen. She finished the letter to Delilah's daughter, signing it as usual with "love," though Delilah never told her to.

10:42 a.m.—Lipscomb Hall, University of Georgia, Athens

Less than thirty minutes after returning to the dorm, Julia awoke to the insistent beeping of her pager. She blindly rummaged in her purse to stop the annoying noise. Her hand got wrapped up in the yellow scarf she'd meant to drop off at the house for her sister. She finally found the button and stopped the beeping.

She rolled onto her back. She stared up at the dorm room ceiling. Her heart was beating so hard that she could feel it in her throat. Julia pressed her fingers to her carotid artery and counted each thump until the ticks slowly wound down to normal.

She had been dreaming about Beatrice Oliver again,

except this time, instead of watching Beatrice from afar, Julia found herself standing in for Beatrice. She was talking to her father—Julia's father—about his toothache, then she was volunteering to go to the store for ice cream, then Julia's mother was giving her some cash, then Julia was walking down the street, only instead of standing in for Beatrice Oliver, she was suddenly Mona No-Name, and it was dark and there was a chill in the air and she saw an old-timey car and then a man's sweaty hand clamped around her mouth and her feet were lifted off the ground and she was dragged into the dark, menacing maw of the open van door.

Julia put her hand to her mouth, wondering what it would feel like to suddenly be silenced. She traced her fingers along her lips, and the touch got lighter and before she knew it, the sweaty, evil man slipped her mind and she was only thinking of Robin. His soft lips pressing against hers. The surprisingly rough texture of his cheek brushing against her neck. His big hands so tender on her breasts, and the feelings this brought because he knew how to touch her. He wasn't grabbing her or twisting her or humping her like a stray dog. He was making love to her.

He was *going* to make love to her. Julia decided it right then and there. Her mother, who seemed to relish having frank and awkward conversations about everything from sex to drugs, had told Julia that it was okay to be intimate with whomever she wanted; the important thing was to make sure that she really wanted to.

Julia really wanted to have sex with Robin Clark.

Not that she needed her mother's permission.

Julia rolled over onto her side. Nancy Griggs, her roommate, had left for pottery class twenty minutes ago. Julia had pretended to be asleep. They had gotten into a huge fight over the weekend because Julia had lectured Nancy about not staying out late at the bars and making sure that someone trustworthy walked her back to the dorm.

Nancy had rolled her eyes, which had made Julia turn strident, which never helped any situation. Even as she yelled at her best friend in the entire world, Julia had been aware that she sounded like her mother. For the first time in her life, she didn't care. Beatrice Oliver probably could've benefited from a strident lecture or two about checking your surroundings, making sure you didn't get snatched off the street by a depraved madman when you walked to the store late at night to get ice cream for your father.

"Go to hell," had been Nancy's clipped response. "Just because you have a boyfriend now doesn't mean you know jack shit."

That was what Nancy was really angry about. Julia had never been in love before (was she in love?). She had never had a steady date (Robin was steady). In their nearly fifteen-year friendship, Nancy had always been the one who had the boyfriends, who was worldly in all the ways that Julia could only read about.

Julia was reminded of one of her grandmother's sayings: Your jump rope has turned into a leash.

"Robin!" Julia bolted up in bed, heart racing again,

too much saliva in her mouth. She grabbed the pager from her purse. Maybe it was Robin. Maybe he was standing by a pay phone in the woods right now waiting for her to call. She pressed the button to make the number scroll. Julia wanted to throw the pager across the room. Not Robin, but probably one of her stupid sisters, who had left the message 55378008, which upside down spelled BOOBLESS.

"Very funny," Julia muttered, thinking at this time of day it had to be her middle sister, Pepper, because her goody-goody baby sister would never miss school.

She swung her legs over the side of the bed, letting her feet tap the floor. She stared at Nancy's messy side of the room. They had bought their sheet sets together at Sears, and picked out the curtains and various posters that decorated the dorm with money they'd both saved from babysitting. Julia could remember how adult they'd felt—they were out on their own! Spending their hard-earned money! Taking care of themselves like real adults!—and then Julia had gone back home and eaten Chinese take-out her parents had paid for and washed the clothes they had paid for in the machine they owned and felt terrified because she really didn't have the ability to support herself at all.

Julia walked two steps and sat down at her desk. She stared at the sheet of notebook paper where she'd started to write a love letter to Robin. She had quoted the Madonna song about kissing in Paris and holding hands in Rome.

Should she really have sex with him? Was Robin the

right guy to do it with? This time last year, Julia would've given it up to just about anybody. Why was it suddenly so special?

She used her pencil to trace the song lyrics.

Kiss you in Paris . . .

Now probably wasn't the best time for a love letter, especially since Robin wouldn't be back until the end of the week. She couldn't be one of those silly girls who dropped their entire lives for a boy. She should be studying for her massive psych final. She should reread her Spenser paper for her noon class with Professor Edwards. She should be honing her story pitch for the *Red & Black* because five weeks had already passed since Beatrice Oliver had been abducted and Julia would have a hard enough time convincing Greg and Lionel and Mr. Hannah that the story was still news.

She tapped her pencil against her mouth. She stared at the Polaroids taped to the wall in front of her: Nancy shooting a bird; her sisters doing bad cartwheels in the park; her parents dancing at a party (slow dancing, but it looked romantic instead of weird); a shot of their turtle, Herschel Walker (an underappreciated Mother's Day gift), sunning himself on the front porch.

A beautiful young girl was walking down the street when suddenly. . .

Julia felt shaken by a thought. Was Beatrice Oliver a virgin, too? Was the person who took her (who was keeping her) the first person she would ever have sex with?

Would he be the last person, too?

"Shut *up!*" a girl yelled down the hallway. Her Alabama twang was muffled through the closed wooden door. She sounded like she was teasing someone, and Julia felt an instant, almost visceral dislike without even laying eyes on her. "No, *you* did it, you goose."

Julia jumped when the door shook. Someone was knocking with a fist.

"Hell-o?" Alabama called.

The dorm was not coed. Julia didn't bother to grab her robe, though she was wearing only a T-shirt and underwear. She regretted the omission when she realized she had never seen the girl before in her life.

That didn't stop the stranger from pushing her way into the room. "What a mess. Y'all need a maid service." Alabama looked under Nancy's bed, then checked the space beside her desk. She went to the closet next.

"I'm sorry," Julia said. "Do I know you?"

"I'm a friend of Nancy's." The girl opened up Nancy's closet. "She said I could borrow her— There it is." She yanked out a leather satchel, displacing piles of shoes. When she turned around, her eyes took in Julia in a slow head-to-toe take-down. "Nice socks."

She left, leaving a sour air of disapproval behind her.

Julia looked down at her socks. They were gray with black and tan dachshunds stitched into the material. She wanted to run into the hall and ask the girl what was wrong with her socks, but she knew that the statement was not about the socks, it was about how the girl could put Julia in her place.

Julia understood these games, but she was at a loss as to how to play them.

She looked at her watch. Her Spenser class didn't start until noon. She still needed to drop off the yellow scarf for her sister. There were also some printouts that her mother had promised to leave on the kitchen table. The sun was shining. The weather was crisp. Maybe a bike ride would clear some of the demons from her head.

Julia pulled on her jeans, threw a sweater over her T-shirt, grabbed her purse, and loaded up her book bag. She had already locked the door when she realized she should've brushed her teeth and run a comb through her hair, but she could do that when she got home. To her parents' home, she meant, because the house on Boulevard wasn't technically where she lived anymore.

Outside the dorm, she wrestled with the lock on her bike, grinding the key through a layer of rust. The morning mist had completely burned off by the time she rode her bicycle past the black iron arch that marked the entrance to the North Campus. She probably should've brought her jacket, but she was all right as long as she stayed in the sunshine. She weaved through the students milling around the center of Broad Street. Their moods seemed light. The weather was caught between winter and spring, and any day that promised sunshine was a day to be celebrated.

The distance between Julia's dorm and the house was less than fifteen minutes, but it always felt like the ride took longer going there than it did coming back. Turning the corner onto the tree-lined streets of her childhood always brought a sense of nostalgia. Julia rose up from her seat as she coasted down Boulevard. The stately Victorians and ranch houses were as familiar to her as the back of her hand. Mostly professors lived in the area, but her mother claimed some of the old-timers had been here since before Jesus lost his sandals.

She nodded to Mrs. Carter, who still kept her garden hose handy in case a kid tried to cut through her wide front yard. She crossed to the opposite side of the street in anticipation of the Bartons' yappy springer spaniel who, no matter how many times he practically choked himself, completely forgot he was chained to a tree every time a person went past.

She turned into the driveway of her parents' yellow Victorian. Pepper's bike was leaned against the front porch, which didn't mean anything because Julia's middle sister was sixteen years old and had plenty of friends who could drive her to school. Her baby sister's pink bike was gone, because perfect little Sweetpea was always exactly where her mother and father expected her to be.

Sweetpea. Julia's youngest sister was neither sweet nor pea-shaped (more like a pointy stick). The nickname had come because she had refused to eat anything but sweet peas the summer she turned eight years old. It was an adorable piece of family lore (like Pepper being called Pepper because Grandma said she had "hell and pepper in her hair") but Julia was the one trapped all summer cranking open a can of peas every time the little brat bellowed for more. Not to mention what happened to the peas on their way out. You would've thought the stupid twerp would've disappeared into a puddle of green diarrhea, but no, she was still around.

Julia felt guilty for that last thought. She should be kinder to her little sister, but it was hard because she had it so much easier than Julia did, as if the five-year age difference had worn her parents down from hard, unmovable boulders into tiny pebbles you could skip across the creek. Of course Julia loved Sweetpea (they were sisters, after all), but sometimes she wanted to strangle her (they were sisters, after all).

To assuage the guilt, Julia reminded herself of the times that they all came together. Like on the rare instances that their parents really argued (*really* argued, because they had heated discussions about a lot of things) and all three girls would sleep in the same bed as if being together would protect them from the shouting. Or when Grandma told Pepper she needed to lose her baby fat and Sweetpea called her a sour old biddy. Or when Julia got arrested the first time she ever tried to smoke pot and both of her sisters stood vigil outside her bedroom door until her parents had finished yelling at her. Or when they all sobbed like babies when Charles and Diana got married because it was so romantic how much they loved each other, and all the Carroll sisters hoped for in life was that their sisters would find the same kind of forever love (preferably with a wealthy prince).

The memories made Julia feel nostalgic as she made her way up to the house. She skipped over the broken porch step (the one her mother yelled at her father to fix) and dodged the pot of dying crocuses (the ones her father yelled at her mother to replant). The front door was unlocked, as usual. No one was sure where a key was, and her mother was reasonably certain that any thief would see the tattered state of their living room furniture and decide there was nothing worth stealing.

Julia's father was a vet. He was constantly bringing home strays, and when her mother put her foot down, Julia and her sisters would start bringing them home. It was not without mild disapproval that the yellow Victorian was known around the neighborhood as the Dr. Dolittle House.

As if on cue, a brown tabby of unknown ownership tangled into Julia's legs as she struggled to put down her book bag. There was a low woof from the couch where Mr. Peterson, a maimed terrier, was recuperating on his back. Ms. Crabapple, a golden Lab with memory issues, was on the floor beside him. The gentle ruminations of a convalescing toucan came from the sunroom.

"Girls, I want you to meet Senora Pincha-Your-Fingers, from the family Ramphastidae," her father had told them, introducing the bird with the usual formality he reserved for patients.

"Ay, caramba," her mother had mumbled, then disappeared into the basement for the rest of the night.

Julia gave the dogs a pet before heading into the kitchen, which was its usual mess. Breakfast plates and dishes were waiting for her sisters to get home from school and wash them (Sweetpea would do it so slowly that finally Pepper would take over). An unfamiliar orange cat jumped onto the counter, a clear violation of her mother's only rule for cats. Julia picked him up and placed him on the floor. The cat jumped back up, but she figured she'd done her part.

She spotted the stack of printouts on the kitchen table. She had asked her mother to find any articles about missing girls in the state of Georgia over the most recent twelve months. The handwriting at the top of the first page was as precise as a kindergarten teacher's, which meant her mother had gotten one of the junior librarians to run the microfiche machine. The woman had written a note: *These are the articles that had no follow-up story re: a return.*

Julia layered some peanut butter onto a banana as she read the first printout. Two months ago, the *Clayton News Daily* had run a front-page story about a girl who had gone missing from the junior college campus. The photograph had printed too dark to get any idea of what the girl looked like, but the description said she was brunette and pretty.

Julia turned the page. The *Statesboro Herald*. Another missing girl, this one last seen at a movie theater. Described as athletic and attractive.

The next article was from the *News Observer*. A missing girl last seen near the Fannin County Fair grounds. Tall with long dark hair and striking features.

The *Tri-County News*. Eden Valley girl reported missing. Blonde hair. Blue eyes. Former beauty queen.

The *Telegraph*. Headline: "Mercer Student's Roommate: She Never Came Home." The student's pastor was quoted in the story. "She is a beautiful, godly young woman, and we all just want her back."

Pretty. Striking. Beautiful. Young.

Like Beatrice Oliver.

Like Mona No-Name.

The two recent disappearances hadn't been archived to the microfiche yet, but in a few months, they would join the inauspicious club. Julia checked the datelines. None of the stories was from Athens, which was a relief for the obvious reason as well as because it meant that she hadn't missed something during her daily read of the *Athens-Clarke Herald*.

Julia stacked the printouts together. The stories had gotten to her. She felt her pulse racing again. The room had turned stuffy. She fanned herself with the papers. They flipped back and forth, offering flash cards of grieving parents and school photos and candid shots taken during summer vacations.

All those pretty girls. All missing. Or taken. Or being kept.

Or maybe their bodies just hadn't been found.

An index card fell out of the pages. This note was in her mother's handwriting—not an admonition for requesting such dark reading material but a dated invoice from the library. Twenty-eight printouts at five cents each.

Julia fished a dollar bill and two quarters out of her purse (annoyingly, her mother would go out of her way to make change). She left the money with the invoice on the table. Her gaze picked out today's date—March 4. Her grandmother's birthday was coming up. Again, Julia dug around in her purse. She found the card she'd bought before Grandma had remarked that Julia looked like she couldn't lose the last five pounds of her "Freshman Fifteen."

"She's calling you fat," Sweetpea had said, helpfully.

Julia tapped the sealed envelope on the table. She had written some nice things inside the birthday card. Nice things that she no longer felt. Could she steam open the envelope and change the sentiment?

In the end, Julia left the card on the table. Maybe this was what taking the high road felt like, but it sure sucked that no one else would ever know about it.

She went into her bedroom, which was on the first floor because her father's upstairs office was too messy to move when Sweetpea had come along. She stood in the doorway, feeling like a stranger even though nothing had changed. The walls were still lilac. Her rock posters were still there—Indigo Girls, R.E.M., Billy Idol on the ceiling so that he was the last thing she looked at when she went to bed at night. Polaroids of high school friends were still stuck in the mirror frame over her dresser. Mr. Biggles was still on the bed. Julia picked up the decrepit stuffed dog and kissed his head, saying her billionth silent apology for accidentally throwing him away the day she packed for college (thank God her father had saved him).

She smoothed back what was left of Mr. Biggles's mangy, patchy fur. The poor thing had suffered his share of slings and arrows. Julia had slept on him so much that he was almost one-dimensional. Sweetpea had trimmed off his hair after a not-so-accidental Kool-Aid spill.

Pepper had singed his nose with a curling iron and Julia had tried to pretend it was funny when, actually, she was dying inside.

Mr. Biggles was gently returned to his rightful place. Julia used the sleeve of her sweater to wipe some dust off the ugly blue lava lamp that she knew her mother despised (which was why Julia had left it here). The orange cat jumped on her bed. Julia ran her hand along his back, then realized that this was a second orange cat. His right leg was shaved where an IV had been inserted. His purr sounded like the vibrating teeth of a comb.

Julia found the yellow scarf in her purse and climbed the stairs to Pepper's bedroom. As usual, the place looked like a bomb had gone off inside. Clothes covered the floor. Books were splayed page-down ("A sin," their mother said). The walls were painted dark gray. The curtains were almost black. That the room felt more like a cave was completely by design. That their mother was infuriated by the effect was also by design.

Julia put her hand to her neck. She had borrowed Pepper's gold locket months ago, but her sister had not noticed that it was missing until last Friday. There had been a heated fight when Julia had claimed she hadn't taken it, then another heated fight when Pepper had realized that Julia was actually wearing the locket and had tucked said locket underneath her shirt to hide it. Instead of giving it back, Julia had stormed out of the house and slammed the door.

"You stole my straw hat!" she had yelled over her shoulder, as if the locket theft was a tit-for-tat.

Why had she been so childish? And why couldn't she just give the locket back now? There was Pepper's makeup vanity spilling over with trinkets that she had worn once, if that, then discarded. Silver and black bangles. A large black bow that actually belonged to Julia. Several T-shirts ripped *Flashdance*-style at the neck. Rainbow-colored leggings. Black tights. More eye shadows and powders and blushes than Julia would ever know what to do with.

Not that her sister needed makeup. If Julia was beautiful, Pepper was voluptuous. (Far more preferable, to Julia's thinking.) Her middle sister was curvy and, now that she was getting older, sensuous in a way that made their father's friends say really stupid things around her.

It wasn't just how Pepper looked. There was something about her attitude that drew people in. She always said what was on her mind. She did whatever she wanted. She didn't worry about what other people thought. She was certainly more experienced than Julia. She'd tried pot in the sixth grade. At a party last week, she'd snorted coke on a dare, which was terrifying if not slightly impressive. The gold locket had been a gift from a boy who had gone all the way with Pepper in the back of his father's Chevy. At least that's what Pepper had said, and why would she lie about something like that?

Julia tucked the locket back under her collar. She slid some of the black and silver bangles over her wrist, because she had bought hers at the same time and there was no telling whose were which. She grabbed the black bow. She left the yellow scarf on the bed, hoping her sister would see it among the discarded clothes. She was turning to leave the room when she heard a low moan.

Julia felt her eyebrows furrow at the familiar noise. Had the poor old Lab gotten stuck in a corner and forgotten how to get out? Was one of the cats about to hork up a hairball?

The moan came again, low and drawn out, kind of like the satisfied sound a person makes when they manage to fully stretch themselves out.

Julia stepped into the hallway. She noticed that her parents' bedroom door was closed. A sliver of light showed around the edges. She heard the moan again and she ran down the stairs before she heard it a fourth time and had to pour acid into her ears to cleanse herself of the memory.

"Yuck," she mumbled, jerking her bike away from the front porch. "Yuck, yuck, yuck."

The entire ride back to campus was filled with thoughts of anything but her parents having sex. The Iran-Contra hearings, which Julia had stayed home from school to watch with her father. The first dog she had, Jim Dandy, a golden retriever with a permanent limp because, as her father said, "Some jackass assumed a dog could understand physics and let him ride untethered in the back of a pick-up truck." Sweetpea's thirteenth birthday party last year, how excited they all were that she was finally a teenager (except for her mother, who drank some of her father's beer and turned maudlin). The way Grandpa Ernie used to pull out his guitar after Sunday dinner and they would all dance to whatever song he was playing, even if no one recognized the tune.

By the time Julia got back to campus, it was exactly noon. She chained up her bike in front of the Tate Student Center and ran to her Spenser class. Professor Edwards was already lecturing at his podium, and he met Julia's harried entrance with a hard stare.

"I'm sorry," she apologized as she made a beeline for her desk in the back. "I forgot my paper and had to go back to my dorm." She started to sit down, but he stopped her.

"Bring it here." He had his hand out. His fingers flexed back and forth, indicating she should move and he was not kidding around.

Julia made the thousand-mile journey back to Professor Edwards. She put her twelve-page paper in his hand. Blots of Wite-Out scabbed the typewritten essay. She started to turn back around, but he said—

"Stay here. This won't take long."

She stood in front of his podium while he read her work. She shifted back and forth from foot to foot. She wrung together her hands. She didn't look at any of the sniggling classmates behind her. Professor Edwards, in turn, did not look at Julia. He had his head down. He flicked the pages with a sharp jerk of his wrist. Sometimes he nodded. More often, he shook his head.

Edwards was younger than most of her teachers, probably in his mid-thirties, but there was a tiny bald spot on top of his head that the girls talked about—not because it made him less attractive (it must be acknowledged that Professor Edwards was very attractive), but because they always knew they could use it as a weapon if he ever tried anything with them.

Because Professor Edwards had a reputation for trying things. It was one of those pieces of advice that got passed down through the classes: Don't walk under the Arch or you won't graduate, SAE stands for "sexual assault expected," don't find yourself alone with Professor Edwards unless you want him to make stray remarks about how pretty you are, what a great ass you have, how your breasts are perfect, or how close his apartment is to campus.

"What's the order of monks who shave their heads in a circle?" Nancy Griggs had asked when they had heard the advice from a graduating senior.

"Franciscan?" Julia had guessed, thinking it was something her mother would know, but that if she told her mother, her father would probably show up at her Spenser class with a shotgun.

"Right," Nancy had said. "When he makes a pass at you, ask him if he's a Franciscan monk because of the bald spot on his head."

When, not *if*. All of the girls assumed that Professor Edwards had a thing for Julia.

The truth was that he'd never made a pass at her, but the rest of the truth was that he didn't have to say anything about her ass or her breasts because his eyes did all of the commenting. The real tragedy (other than that he got away with it) was that Edwards was actually a great teacher. Julia had coasted through high school on her writing. Edwards challenged her to put more effort into her work. He spotted her bullshit from miles away. He rewrote her sentences, explaining the rhetorical difference. He made her want to be better.

And at the same time, he made her extremely uncomfortable.

Edwards finally looked up from her essay. "I like where you're going with this, but you know it needs work."

"Yes, sir."

He held her gaze. Her paper was still on the podium, one of his big hands holding it down in case she tried to take it.

Julia gripped together her hands. Her face was flushed. She was sweating. She hated any kind of attention, and the worst part was that she sensed that Professor Edwards understood this, and was torturing her for it just because he could.

"All right." He clicked his pen and started marking up the pages with quick strokes that cut into the pulp of the paper. "Don't need this—" He slashed an X through two paragraphs she had spent hours on. "And this—" He circled another paragraph, then drew an arrow up to the top of the page. "Move it here, then move this here. And, actually, this paragraph on the back page should move up to the beginning, right around here, and this is redundant. This, too. This I like, but just barely."

By the time he was finished, both Julia and her paper were reminiscent of an Escher clock spiraling into despair.

"Understand?" Edwards asked.

"Yes, sir." She understood that she was never to be late for another class ever again.

Julia took the paper. He held on to it a second longer than necessary, so when she finally wrested it from his grip, the pages fluttered. She pretended to thumb through his notes as she walked back to her desk. She could feel Edwards watching her every move, and he even gave a weird grunt when she sat down at her desk, like he was mimicking the opening of an Al Green song.

1:20 p.m.—Tate Student Center, University of Georgia, Athens

Julia sat across the table from Veronica Voorhees, who was supposed to be sharing her salad but had already eaten over half of it. Julia didn't care. Her stomach was upset from the run-in with Professor Edwards—not the one at the beginning of class, but the one after class was over.

Julia had been the last to leave the room. Suddenly, Edwards was right behind her, so close that she could feel his hot breath on her neck when he whispered, "Extra credit if I see you at my lecture tonight."

"Oh," she said, momentarily stunned by the closeness. "Okay."

"South Campus. We could get coffee afterward, maybe talk about your paper some more."

"S-s-sure," she had stuttered like an idiot.

And then she'd felt his palm smooth the curve of her ass the same admiring way that she'd seen men at live-stock auctions run their hand over an animal's flank.

Julia was two floors down the stairs before she started to brim with should'ves. She should've slapped away his hand. She should've asked him what the hell he was doing. She should've told him to leave her alone, that he was disgusting, that he was cruel, that he was a really good teacher, so why the hell did he have to make everything gross by being such a creep?

"What're you so pensive about?" Veronica asked. Salad fell out of her mouth. She reminded Julia of how Mona No-Name ate the first day she showed up at the shelter. She had shoveled in so much food that she started to choke.

Mona. Julia had been so wrapped up in her petty problems with Professor Edwards that she had forgotten all about the missing homeless girl.

Was Mona really missing? Had a man really snatched her off the street and dragged her into his van? Had that same van pulled to a stop behind Beatrice Oliver five weeks ago? Whoever took either or both women knew what he was doing. He wasn't a bogeyman or a cartoon wolf. He was a shark with razor-sharp teeth who snatched helpless women from the surface and dragged them down to a dark place where he could devour them.

"Julia?" Veronica knocked on the table for attention. "What's going on with you, kid?"

"Just tired." Julia took a bite of grilled cheese sandwich to give her mouth something to do. She tried to banish the shark images from her mind by letting her thoughts return to Professor Edwards.

She could report him, but whoever took her complaint would give Edwards a chance to respond. Julia had no doubt he would have a good response. She ticked all of the boxes quickly: *She's mad because I gave her a bad grade on her paper. This is payback because she threw herself at me and I said no. She's crazy. She's a bitch. She's a liar. She's been in trouble before.*

That last bit was actually true. Julia had been detained by the campus police last year. Some of the graduating seniors at the *Red & Black* had dared Julia to do something more than write a damning op-ed about the agricultural college's foray into genetically modified organisms. She hadn't realized that she was the only person *not* on speed until after they'd all broken into the lab and destroyed some equipment.

"Their pupils are bigger than my dick," the campus cop had told his partner.

Julia had never seen a real penis before, but she'd had no doubt that he was correct. In the cold light of the cop's flashlight, her fellow criminals were obviously stoned out of their minds.

"Hey, beautiful!" Ezekiel Mann stood behind Julia's chair. His clammy hands rubbed her shoulders. "Where did you go?"

Julia hadn't gone anywhere, but she said, "Sorry."

"No problem." His fingers dug into her skin. "You got time for that game of pool?"

Julia was standing up before he finished the sentence. She had been manhandled enough for the day.

"Ladies first." He placed a cue stick in her hand.

Julia took the stick because people were watching and she didn't want to seem rude. She was really good at pool (her grandmother had taught her) but she purposefully missed even the easiest shots so that Ezekiel wouldn't be embarrassed. The only saving grace was David Conford, sitting on one of the tweedy, overstuffed couches, who called the game like he was Howard Cosell.

"Julia Carroll, a young kid with a glint in her eye, leans across the table. Will she go for the six or the ten?" David stopped to drink from his bottle of Coke. He dropped out of character. "You know, Julia, you're really bad at this."

Ezekiel said, "She's pretty. She doesn't need to be good at anything."

Julia changed her angle and banked the six and ten ball into the corner pocket.

"*Down goes Frazier!*" David clapped his hands together. "The comeback kid stuns the crowd."

To David's further delight, Julia sank the last four balls, then put the eight in the side pocket while Ezekiel stood slack-jawed, his cue stick in front of him like a scaled-down petard.

Julia sat by David on the arm of the couch. "That was fun."

Ezekiel jammed his stick into the rack and stomped away.

David laughed good-naturedly as his departing friend. He told Julia, "Hey, Fast Eddie, gimme a heads-up next time so I can place a smacker on the game."

She laughed, because David was one of those boys who was effortlessly funny.

He said, "I hear Michael Stipe is going to be at the Manhattan tonight."

"Right." There were daily rumors that the lead singer

of R.E.M. was going to be in this bar or the next one to-night or this weekend or maybe he was already there. "I thought he was on tour?"

"Just calls 'em likes I sees 'em, sweetheart." David got up from the couch. "Maybe I'll see you there."

"Maybe," Julia said, but just to be nice.

The student center was clearing out. Julia grabbed her purse and her book bag. Instead of getting on her bike, she headed toward the *Red & Black* offices a few buildings away. She felt buoyed by the pool game (she had let herself win at something!) and she wanted to take advantage of the slight boost to her ego and present her pitch for the Beatrice Oliver story.

The twenty-eight printouts her mother left on the kitchen table had brought the focus of Julia's pitch to a fine point. People always said they wanted hard news, but what they really wanted was to be scared. These girls were all so normal. So innocent. So familiar. They could've been your mother or your cousin or your girlfriend. A daughter vanishes from a movie theater. A sister disappears at the fairgrounds. A beloved aunt drives off in her car and is never seen again. Julia knew what mattered in Beatrice's story—the same details that had haunted her all these weeks.

A beautiful girl disappeared while getting ice cream for her ailing father...

Julia smiled. She repeated the line to herself as she walked down the long hallway to the *Red & Black* of-fices. And then she coughed in the perpetual hazy film of smoke that drifted out of the open doorway. They were all supposed to be reporters, but no one was about to do a story on the dangers of secondhand smoke because their advisor would rather take early retirement than give up his Marlboro Reds.

Mr. Hannah called the journalism room his bullpen, which seemed to Julia a glorified way of saying he wasn't going to clean the mounds of papers from his desk, from the corners, and especially from the loaded bookshelves that ran around the periphery of the room.

Julia loved the mess. She loved the horrible smells— the nicotine and ink and that weird blue stuff that came out of the mimeograph machine. She loved the clacking of the telex and the whir of the printer and the shush of Spray Mount and zwip of the paper cutter and the hum of the two Macintosh computers on the long table at the back of the room. She especially loved Mr. Hannah because he had worked at the *New York Times*, the *Atlanta Constitution* and the *L.A. Times* all before pissing off so many people that the only place left to spout off his big mouth was inside the halls of academia.

"Tenure," he often told them, "is the last bastion of free speech."

Despite his scraggly, unkempt appearance, Mr. Hannah had done pretty well by moving to Athens. UGA's Grady College of Journalism was nationally re-nowned, which was fantastic if you were a parent who didn't want to pay out-of-state tuition and horrible if you were an aspiring journalism student who wanted to live somewhere other than the town in which you grew up.

Mr. Hannah smiled when Julia walked into the room. "There's my pretty girl." Somehow, he made the words seem like a gesture of affection rather than a creepy come-on. "Where is my riveting piece on the coming privatization of the cafeteria's meal services?"

Julia handed him her article. He scanned it while she stood there, the overhead light reflecting her typed words back onto the lenses of his eyeglasses.

"It works," he said, which was the best any of them could ever hope for. "What else you got for me? I need some news."

"I was thinking," Julia began, even as she felt the opening line she had so deftly crafted just moments ago slip out of her brain and float into the ether. "A girl—a beautiful girl—was . . . and . . ."

Mr. Hannah clapped together his hands. "And?"

"And . . ." Julia's skull was an empty, brainless Tupperware bowl. She was vibrating with anxiety. She felt like she was going to burst into tears.

"Julia?"

"Yes." She cleared her throat. Her tongue had turned into a bag of wet salt. She went to the facts, because the facts mattered. "There's a girl who disappeared. She lives—lived—about fifteen minutes from here."

"And?"

"Well, she's gone. Abducted. The detective on the case said—"

"Probably ran off with a boyfriend," someone interrupted.

Julia looked over Mr. Hannah's shoulder. Greg Gianakos. Lionel Vance. Budgy Green. Their heads stuck up above the production partition like prairie dogs. They all had cigarettes dangling from their mouths, and all were on their way to becoming as flabby and bleary-eyed as their mentor. The only difference was that they looked at her with a marked absence of Mr. Hannah's kindness.

"Ignore them, kid," Mr. Hannah coaxed. "Pitch me a story I can put on the front page."

"Okay," Julia said, like it was that easy to recapture her earlier certainty. What was the heart of the Beatrice Oliver story? What was the hook? Julia thought about the terror that had gripped her when she first read about the girl's abduction on the telex. The menace she had felt this morning when she walked down streets that were as familiar as her childhood home. The fear summoned by the articles she'd read in her mother's kitchen. She had to distill for Mr. Hannah what really bothered her about the Beatrice Oliver abduction. It wasn't *just* that the girl was snatched off the street. It wasn't *just* that she was being kept. It was why she had been taken in the first place.

She told Mr. Hannah, "Rape."

"Rape?" He was obviously surprised. "What about it?"

"She was raped," Julia said, because why else would a man abduct a woman less than two blocks from her family home? Why else would he keep her?

"Are you talking about Jenny Loudermilk?" Greg Gianakos stood up from his desk. He crossed his arms over his broad chest. "No way you can squeeze more than a paragraph out of that."

Julia shrugged, but only because she had no idea who Jenny Loudermilk was.

Apparently, neither did Mr. Hannah. "Fill me in."

"Sophomore," Greg said, though Mr. Hannah had directed his request to Julia. "Good-looking blonde. Wrong place, wrong time."

Lionel Vance took over. "I heard she was pretty sloppy. Spent most of the night looking for the bottom of a PBR."

"Yeah, everybody knows sophomores are cheap drunks." Greg was clearly annoyed at having his story stepped on. "Anyway, the gal was pouring her way down Broad Street and some guy grabbed her, took her into an alley, and raped her."

Mr. Hannah patted his pockets for his cigarettes. "Nobody wants to read about rape. Say assaulted, or attacked, or threatened if she wasn't hit." He asked Julia, "That's the story you want to tell?"

"Well, I—"

"She won't talk to you," Lionel said. "The victim. They never talk. So, what's your story? Some girl gets drunk and goes off with the wrong guy? Like Greg said, that's barely a paragraph. I wouldn't even put it on the back page."

Mr. Hannah lit his cigarette. He asked Julia, "You agree? Disagree?"

"I think—"

"It's an anomaly," Greg interrupted. "If your story is that suddenly the world is filled with rapists, you're wrong. And a university campus is statistically one of the safest places to be."

Mr. Hannah blew out a stream of smoke. "Statistics, huh?"

Greg said, "Look, Jules. Don't let your emotions cloud your judgment. Yes, what happened to Jenny shouldn't have happened, but a reporter only reports the facts, and you won't get any facts here because the victim already scurried off home, the guy who did it certainly won't talk, and the cops won't discuss a case that's never going to be prosecuted."

Julia's fingernails dug into her palms. She thought about the stack of printouts in her purse. She wanted to throw them in Greg's smug face, but they would only prove his point. Twenty-eight women in a state with a population of almost 6.5 million was hardly a significant number.

He seemed to read her mind. "Jenny Loudermilk was one girl out of approximately fifteen thousand female students. That's an outlier."

Julia tried, "It doesn't always get reported."

"Because half of them got drunk and changed their minds."

"I meant reported in the newspaper." She remembered that the articles were about missing women, not women who had been raped. Assaulted. Attacked. "Or reported to the police. Or reported to anybody."

"For good reason." Greg lit a cigarette. "This is the story: that the campus is safer for women than it's ever been. That the world is safer for women than it's ever been."

"Is that right?" Mr. Hannah crossed his arms over his

chest. He was grinning like a maniac. "Back that up, hot-shot. Gimme your statistical proof that the world is safer for women, other than because it looks great through your Wonder Bread View-Master."

"I will." Greg went to one of the Macintoshes at the back of the room. He turned on the machine and sat down. "We've got all the crime statistics from the last ten years on a set of discs."

"I'm gonna die of old age by the time that thing boots up." Mr. Hannah stood at the metal shelves behind his desk. He traced his finger along the spines of several books until he found what he was looking for. "The FBI is mandated by the United States Congress to collect all relevant crime data from a set number of police forces around the country at least once every year." He plucked out several books. "The most current report I've got is 1989."

He handed one of the volumes to Julia.

"Budgy," Mr. Hannah called to the only boy who hadn't joined the fray. "Get thee to the chalkboard. We need a non-English major for our computations. Julia—" He gave Julia a nod. "Population of the United States in 1989?"

She cracked open the book and thumbed through the index. She found the page number, then the correct page, and read, "It was 252,153,092."

"Half that, Budgy. Men don't count in this equation."

"It's not half," Budgy said. "Women are slightly less than fifty-one percent of the population."

"L'chaim." Mr. Hannah tapped his cigarette ash into

a Styrofoam cup. "But half whatever you get from your fifty-one percent, because they don't collect data below the age of consent."

Julia thought she'd heard wrong. She looked down at the book in her lap and ran her finger down to the methodology. *Forcible rape includes assaults or attempts to commit rape by force or threat of force; however, statutory rape (without force) and other sex offenses are excluded.*

"You should half that number a third time," Greg said. "At least that many women have buyer's remorse."

"Whoa there." Mr. Hannah held up his hand like a referee calling a foul. "No conjecture allowed. Let's stick to the data." He instructed Julia, "So, in your story, you'll say, 'Extrapolating from the FBI's Uniform Crime Reports blah-blah-blah,' right?"

Julia nodded, but this had stopped being her story a while ago.

Mr. Hannah asked, "Number of reported assaults in 1989? Julia?"

"Oh, sorry." Julia looked for the correct column. "Forcible rapes: 106,593."

"All right. 106,593," Mr. Hannah repeated, making sure Budgy got the number right. "That's probably pretty consistent across the last five years, but we'll need to verify that."

Julia stared at the board, boggled by the figure. The population of Athens-Clarke County was less than one hundred thousand. The statistic was greater than every single person in town—man, woman, and child.

"Come on, Budgy. Work the chalk." Mr. Hannah

clapped his hands to get Budgy moving. "Round up, son. We don't have all day."

Julia checked the data a second time, certain she'd seen it wrong. There it was: 106,593. She stared at the numbers until they blurred. Over one hundred thousand women. And that was just the ones who were over the age of consent. And had actually reported the crime. And had been threatened with violence. What were the other sex offenses that didn't count? What about the women who didn't go to the police?

Why did the crime only make the newspapers if the girl wasn't around to tell her story?

"Got it." Budgy underlined the number so many times that the chalk broke in two. "At the current levels, women in the United States have a .0434 percent chance of being assaulted. That's around forty-three per one hundred thousand."

Mr. Hannah was as familiar with the population number of Athens as Julia was. He summed up, "So, transferring that number to our own fair city, that's roughly twenty-two women a year, which is around one assault every two and a half weeks."

Julia closed the book. Were Beatrice Oliver and Mona No-Name two victims for the list? Jenny Loudermilk made three. Setting aside that it was already March and there were probably others, that left at least nineteen more Athens women who would be raped before 1992 rolled in.

And then the clock would reset and the countdown would start all over.

Greg spiked his cigarette into a Coke can. "Less than

half of one percent seems pretty rare to me." He crossed his arms over his chest. "You'd have a better chance getting struck by lightning or winning the lottery."

Budgy laughed. "You sure about that, Einstein?"

"Figure of speech." Greg waved away the sarcasm, asking Julia, "Why did you want to do this story again? That's like, a hundred thousand people out of almost three hundred million—a drop in the bucket. Nobody cares about that. It's not news."

Julia wasn't given time to answer.

"What about murder?" Lionel took the book from Julia. "Let's do murder. I wanna know my chances."

"Pretty high if your parents find out you're failing trig." Budgy grabbed the chalk. "Okay, population goes back up to 252 million—"

"AIDS," Julia said.

They all turned to look at her.

"You said it didn't matter because it's only a hundred thousand people." She willed her voice to remain steady. "Around the same number of U.S. AIDS cases were diagnosed in 1989, but the story's on the cover of *Time*, *Newsweek*... every newspaper in the country has some kind of story every day, and the president gives speeches about it, Congress does hearings, the Americans with Disabilities Act ensures—"

"People can't lie about having AIDS," Greg interrupted.

Julia felt a bolt of fire pass through her body. "If you want to speculate, then speculate that the handful of liars are more than canceled out by all the women who never come forward, or the women who are underage, or the women who weren't beaten during—"

"The surgeon general of the United States has called AIDS an epidemic." Greg's tone was infuriatingly pedantic. "And you don't say diagnosed with AIDS, you say diagnosed with HIV, the virus that causes AIDS."

Julia mumbled a rare curse under her breath.

Greg pretended not to hear her. "And also, people die from AIDS. Women don't die from assault."

Lionel said, "Part of their vaginas do."

"Hey." Budgy threw the eraser at his head. "Don't be an asshole."

Mr. Hannah asked Julia, "What's the lede?"

She didn't have to think about it this time. "Something horrible happens to at least a hundred thousand American women every single year, and no one seems to care about it."

Greg snorted. "I'm sure *Cosmo* is all over it."

Mr. Hannah made a swipe of his hand to shut him up. He told Julia, "Keep boiling it down."

"In news reporting, when something bad happens predominantly to males, it's an epidemic worth national attention, but when something bad happens to women—"

"Oh, come on," Greg groaned. "Why does it always have to come down to how shitty men are?"

"It's not—"

"We get it," Greg said. "You're a feminist."

"I didn't—"

"You hate us because we have dicks."

"Stop interrupting me!" The sound of Julia's fist slamming against the desk echoed like a gunshot. "I don't hate you because you have a dick. I hate you because you *are* a dick."

The room went utterly and completely silent.

Julia took a stuttered breath, as if she'd just poked her head up above the water.

"Oh, burn!" Lionel punched Greg in the arm. "Score one for the ice queen!"

"She didn't—" Greg said. "It's not—"

Julia spun on her heel and headed toward the door. Her hands were shaking. She felt trembly and annoyed and, underneath, slightly proud of herself because what a fantastic parting shot.

"Hey." Mr. Hannah caught up with her in the hallway.

Julia turned around. "I'm sorry I—"

"Good reporters never apologize."

"Oh," she said, because nothing more cogent came to mind.

"I want the draft of that story on my desk by ten Friday morning."

Julia's mouth opened. Nothing came out. She had stopped breathing again. She needed to breathe.

"That do-able?"

"Yes," she said. "I also have—I mean—I can—"

"Put it in your article. Twelve hundred words."

"Twelve hundred is the—"

"Front page." He winked at her. "You got this, kid."

She watched him cut through the thick smoke as he returned to the bullpen.

The front page.

Panic set in the moment she started walking down the hallway. Julia put her fingers to her neck. Her pulse was ticking like a bomb. Her vision tunneled to the light coming through the glass doors thirty yards away.

Mr. Hannah said that she had it, but what exactly did she have? Beatrice Oliver's story wasn't tied up in this new one. Not really. Beatrice was gone. She had probably been abducted (the detective had said as much) but anything past that was speculation. Ditto for the printouts in Julia's purse about the twenty-eight missing women. They had vanished. That's all anyone could say about them. They were young, they were beautiful, they were striking, and they were gone.

How was that news?

"Jesus," she mumbled. It wasn't news. At least not enough news.

This was what Julia got for running her mouth without thinking. She had been so flustered, and so angry, and so tired of being talked over and dismissed, and Greg had taken a stray comment and goat-roped her into a loaded political commentary when all Julia was really saying was that it was a story when something—anything— happened to one hundred thousand people every single year.

But why in the hell had she said that AIDS only affected men when Delilah was a perfect contradiction?

She hadn't said it *only* affected men. She'd said it *predominantly* affected men, and she hadn't said rape was worse than AIDS, she'd said that it was awful on its own without any other comparisons and that no one wanted to write about it. No one even wanted to call it what it really was. *Assaulted. Attacked. Threatened.* No wonder Jenny Loudermilk had left town. How could any woman talk about something horrible that had happened to her if she wasn't even allowed to call it by its real name?

That was the story. A crime without a name. Victims without a voice.

Julia pulled a notepad and pen out of her book bag. She needed to write some of this down before she forgot it.

"What's poppin', soda?"

She almost dropped her pen. Robin was leaning against the wall. His hands were in his pockets. He was wearing a flannel shirt and acid-washed jeans and his hair was a mess.

Julia felt a silly grin break across her face. "I thought you were camping this week."

"My little sister forgot her asthma inhaler." He grinned back. "She's got enough to last until tonight."

"That's nice. I mean, nice that you got it for her."

"I haven't been by the house yet." He leaned down, letting his forehead touch hers. "I was hoping I would run into you."

Her heart flopped in her chest. "How did you know I was here?"

"I asked around."

"Oh."

"You look pretty."

She should've combed her hair. And brushed her teeth. And worn something nicer. And lost five pounds (damn her stupid grandmother).

"Look." Robin held her hand like he was admiring a piece of china. "I don't know if this is the right thing or wrong thing to say, but my entire family is out in the woods right now and the house is empty, and they don't expect me back for at least another two hours, and I'd really like to spend some time alone with you."

She nodded, and then her heart flopped again when she realized why it mattered that his parents' house was empty and he had two hours to fill.

He touched his nose to hers. "Does that sound like a good idea?"

Julia was speechless again for all the wrong reasons. This morning, she'd been so certain that she was ready for this, but now, she felt the early tremors of an anxiety attack. Could she really do this? *Should* she really do this? Would Robin still want to be with her if she gave in to him? And could she call it giving in to him if it was something she wanted, too?

Because she wanted it. Even underneath her panic, she knew that she wanted it.

So did that mean she was a bad girl, or a liberated woman, or a prick tease, or a slut? This was so much more than sex. It was about whether she did too much or didn't do enough, or knew how things worked or didn't know what went where.

Okay, that was crazy. Of course she knew the basics—the what goes where—but there were other things to do, to use, to touch or put in your mouth or to lick or bite (or was her sister lying about that? Because it sounded painful) and the fact was that Julia was nineteen years old and she had no idea what she was doing. For the love of God, she hid her birth control pills inside a shoe at the back of her closet because she didn't want Nancy Griggs to tell everyone that she was loose.

Robin asked, "You okay?"

Julia pressed his hand over her heart, which was pounding out a nagging drumbeat of terror because even on the Pill, she could get pregnant, and even with a condom, she might catch something horrible, and her life would be over and she would never see her name under the *Atlanta Journal* masthead or be able to report on camera from a devastating tornado, so why the hell would she take such an extraordinarily idiotic risk in the first place?

"It's okay." Robin gave her a crooked half smile. "Seriously, if you don't want to—"

"Yes," she said. "I want to."

4:20 p.m.—Outside the Tate Student Center, University of Georgia, Athens

Julia's fingers were still trembling when she dropped a quarter into the pay phone. Her mouth felt bruised from Robin's kisses. Her breasts tingled. She could still feel him inside of her. She felt like there was a big neon sign over her head that read JULIA CARROLL: LOVED.

She wanted to sing. She wanted to dance. She wanted to stand in the middle of the quad and toss her hat high into the air.

Pepper answered the phone on the second ring. "Carroll residence."

"Hey, it's me."

"Oh, God, I'm so glad you called." Pepper's voice became muffled. "Can you still hear me?"

Julia glanced around as if someone might be listening. "What is it?"

"The Brat got detention."

Julia momentarily forgot about Robin. "Are you lying?"

"No. She's fine, but Angie Wexler tried to jump her in the hall after school."

Julia put her hand to her mouth. Poor Sweetpea.

"Don't feel sorry for her," Pepper said. "Mom and Dad aren't even going to punish her."

Julia felt her sympathy drain away.

"She told them it was because she wouldn't let Angie cheat off her chemistry lab, but what really happened is that Angie caught the Brat making out with her brother. Who is seventeen years old and has a car."

Julia was so glad that she finally had more experience with boys than her stupid baby sister. "Is she okay?"

"She's acting all sad so that Mom and Dad will feel sorry for her. They're still going to Harry Bissett's tonight."

"I thought Mom said the waiters were too ironic?"

"It's Athens. Everybody's too ironic. Why did you call?"

Julia picked at a strip of peeling paint on the pay phone. There was a lump in her throat. She blinked away the sudden tears that had come into her eyes. Why was she crying?

"Are you okay?"

"Of course." Julia wiped her eyes. "Tell me about your day."

Pepper launched into a litany of complaints—about their parents, their sister, her teachers at school.

Julia stared up at the cloudless blue sky. She had called to tell Pepper about Robin, but now she wasn't sure that she was ready to share. What had happened between them was special, and romantic, and beautiful, and plea- surable (she was pretty sure she'd orgasmed), but gossip- ing about it seemed wrong, especially on a pay phone. She would tell Pepper next month, after it had happened more than once (and when she was sure she'd orgasmed). She would mention it casually, like, "Oh, *that*. Of course we've done *that*."

"Anyway," Pepper said. "That freaky girl with the googly eyes is coming over to study with the Brat. I'll probably go practice with the band."

"I'll probably be at the Manhattan," Julia said, be- cause Robin had told her that he might be able to sneak off tonight after his parents went to sleep. There was a pay phone near the ranger station. He would page Julia with three ones if he could make it and three twos if he couldn't. The thought of waiting around her dorm room for her pager to beep was excruciating.

"Hey, space cadet, you there?" Pepper sounded exas- perated. "I asked if you borrowed my bangles."

Julia lifted her wrist. The silver and black bangles slid down her arm. "Check the Brat's room."

"I'll do it later. She's really upset." Pepper lowered her

voice again. "And you better believe I'm going to swing by Angie Wexler's house tonight and scare the shit out of that little snot-nosed bitch. And her stupid pedophile brother."

"Good." Julia leaned her head against the wall. Pepper was so much better at intimidating people. Julia much preferred to stay in the background and offer silent encouragement. "Hey, do you ever wonder what's gonna happen to us when we're old?"

Pepper barked a surprised laugh. "Where did that come from?"

Julia knew where it had come from. Being held by Robin, seeing the way he looked at her, listening to him talk about how he liked working at the bakery, and maybe if his art career didn't take off, he could see himself working with his dad, maybe one day teaching his own son the business.

His own son.

Julia could give him that. She wanted to give him that. When they were ready.

She told Pepper, "Like, twenty years from now, what're our lives going to be like?"

"Talking about hemorrhoids and trading tips on how to keep our dentures clean."

"Do the math, dipshit. We'll be Mom's age."

"Mom wears orthopedic shoes."

Julia groaned. She was right, but they were too cool to get old like that.

Pepper said, "You'll be married to a great guy who loves you and I'll be divorced from an asshole who left me when his music career took off."

Julia smiled, because Pepper might be right. "The Brat will be married to some computer geek who worships the ground she walks on and has at least half a million dollars in the bank."

"She'll probably cheat on him with my asshole ex."

"You could be the asshole who leaves her husband when *her* music career takes off."

"Maybe," Pepper said, but she didn't sound convinced.

"Listen." Julia glanced around again to make sure no one could hear her. "About the coke . . ."

"I know."

She didn't know. Julia had seen it happen—first to a friend in high school, then to a junior who dropped out of college and ended up at the shelter. "It can go from being fun to being a problem really fast."

"Don't worry, we've got a topflight homeless shelter in town."

"Lydia."

Pepper was quiet. No one ever called her by her real name. "I'd better go. I told Her Highness I would bring her some cocoa."

"Kiss her for me."

Pepper made a smacking sound and hung up.

Julia left her hand on the receiver long after the call had ended. Pepper liked cocaine. She had used it twice since that fateful party. She liked pills. She liked being with the band. She liked checking out and floating into the oblivion and she especially liked doing it when there was a cute guy around.

It wouldn't be a problem, though. Julia would make

sure of that. Her sister was a free spirit. She was going through a phase, like when Julia refused to wear anything that was orange, or when the Brat would eat only sweet peas.

Julia closed her eyes, and let a vision wash over her: sitting on the back porch of the Boulevard house, Pepper and Sweetpea playing cards on the steps, her parents in their rocking chairs, children running in the yard. *Their* children—Pepper, Julia, even the Brat, who would have one perfect, golden child who ended up curing cancer shortly after refusing a third term as president of the United States.

Julia wanted her children to be close to her sisters' children. She wanted them to feel the same connection she felt with her family. The same safety. The same love. Nothing bad happened to people who were connected to their families. Maybe that had been Beatrice Oliver's problem. The first telex story had reported that the missing girl was an only child. Wouldn't it have been different if she'd had sisters? Wouldn't a sister have gone with Beatrice to get ice cream and complain about what happened at school that day? Wouldn't a baby sister have pitched a fit so she could tag along, too?

Julia could only imagine Beatrice's mother's sleepless nights as she ran though the if-onlys: *If only I had gone to the store instead. If only I had driven her. If only we'd had more children so that the loss of one would be mitigated by the presence of the others.*

Could that kind of loss be mitigated, though? Julia couldn't imagine what it was like to lose a child. The loss of a beloved pet, even a gerbil or ferret, brought her entire family (including her mother) to their knees. They would cry in front of the TV, sob at the dinner table, mourn as they cuddled all of the remaining dogs and cats and various creatures around themselves in a big, furry blanket.

No one would mourn the loss of Mona No-Name. No one but Julia, whose imagination would not stop running wild. Was Mona being kept like Beatrice Oliver? Or maybe Mona's situation was more like Jenny Loudermilk's, the girl who'd decided after being attacked that it was easier to just disappear.

No matter what, didn't part of a girl automatically disappear when something bad like that happened? Didn't a rapist take away the girl—the woman—she was going to be and replace her with someone who was afraid for the rest of her life? Even if Beatrice Oliver was freed (even if she was still alive), how could she go back home after being raped? How would she be able to look her father in the eye? How could she not wince for the rest of her life every time a man, even a good man, looked at her?

Julia wiped underneath her eyes with the tips of her fingers. Maybe Greg Gianakos was right about letting your emotions get in the way of a story.

She found her bicycle still chained to the rack, but she couldn't jam the stupid key into the rusted lock. Julia shoved her hands into her pockets and trudged back toward her dorm. The grounds crew was working on a section of lawn that had been destroyed by a group of rugby players. Julia gave the men a wide berth, holding her breath as the smell of fertilizer filled her nostrils. She tried to map out the rest of her night. She should take a sleeping bag to the library. She had to study for her psych exam. She needed to redo her Spenser paper. She needed to find some more statistics for her story. Her *front-page* story. God, what had she gotten herself into? A draft by Friday? She'd be lucky if she had an outline.

"You going back?" Nancy asked. She had come out of nowhere. She laughed when she saw Julia startle. "It's just me, silly."

"Let's go out tonight." Worrying about everything tomorrow sounded like a really good idea. "I heard Michael Stipe is going to be at the Manhattan."

Nancy's eyes narrowed. "I heard he was supposed to be at the Grit. Or was it the Georgia Bar?"

"We can still have fun. Maybe meet some cute guys. Get them to buy us some drinks."

Nancy bumped her hip. "I thought you already had a cute guy."

Julia smiled, and blushed, and felt relieved, because she could tell that the tension between them was over. "Let's get a group together. It'll be fun."

"I dunno. I need to study."

"We'll go to the library, then we'll get something to eat, then we'll meet everybody around nine-thirty tonight." The time wasn't completely random. Robin had promised he would call her pager by ten. Three twos would mean that he couldn't sneak away, in which case it would be nice to be at a noisy bar where she could drink and dance away her crushing disappointment.

And if he sent three ones, then she would be closer to his parents' house, which would still be vacant, and would be vacant for the rest of the night.

"Whattaya say?" Julia asked, because most of her friends were really Nancy's friends. "Sounds fun, right?"

Nancy smiled. "Sounds awesome."

9:46 p.m.—The Manhattan Café, downtown Athens, Georgia

Julia loved dancing, mostly because she was terrible at it. People stopped to watch. They looked at her not because she was attractive, but because she was making a fool of herself.

As her father said about almost every one of her previous boyfriends, it was hard to dislike a fool.

"Did you see Top Gun?" Nancy nodded toward a lesser Tom Cruise standing at the bar. Julia squinted her eyes to see through the thick layer of cigarette smoke. The man wore a bomber jacket and sunglasses, even though it was warm and he was inside.

"Foxy," Julia said, trying to keep as much of the beat as she could. Her dancing was never enhanced by trying to carry on a conversation. The floor was packed. People kept bumping into her, or maybe she was the one who kept bumping into them. After getting elbowed in the ribs, she finally gave up and nodded for Nancy to follow her to the bathroom.

The line was packed with students, most of them underage. Julia recognized the snippy girl from this morning who'd borrowed Nancy's leather satchel and insulted Julia's socks. Alabama was clearly out of it. She was swaying back and forth, catching herself at the last second before she fell flat on her face. No one was helping her. Maybe she'd insulted their socks, too.

"Jesus," Nancy said. "Have some dignity."

Julia had to raise her voice over the music. "Do you know her?"

"Deanie Crowder." Nancy rolled her eyes in a way that indicated she wished that she didn't.

"I hope she's got somebody to take her home." Julia felt her strident voice start to simmer in the back of her throat. Jenny Loudermilk had gone home alone and look what had happened to her.

"Why do you keep looking at your watch?"

Julia looked up from her watch. "No reason. Just feels later than it is." She had her pager on vibrate, but still she checked it.

"Who's supposed to call?"

"Sorry. My little sister got in trouble today."

"The Golden Child?"

"She's not so bad." Julia clipped the pager back on the inside of her pocket. She should've called Sweetpea to check in on her. And she should've been firmer with Pepper about the drugs. She was the big sister. It was her job to look out for them. She would find time for both of them this weekend. Maybe take Sweetpea to Wuxtry to buy an album. She really wasn't that bad once you got her alone.

"Move!" somebody called from the back of the line.

They inched closer to the bathroom. Julia saw herself in a floor-length mirror. She was wearing one of Robin's shirts. He'd pulled it out of the laundry basket for her. She put her hand to her neck and found Pepper's locket. The silver and black bangles fell down her arm. She would give the locket back this weekend. And the bangles. And the straw hat, because it was Pepper's anyway.

"You look great," Nancy said. "No, wait, you look byoootiful."

Julia laughed. She was imitating the goofy guy at the Taco Stand who flirted with every girl who walked through the door.

Nancy asked, "How about me?"

"You look byoootiful, too." Nancy actually looked pretty good. She had chosen to go Cyndi Lauper to Julia's Madonna. Her dark hair was spiked up. She wore a multicolored bolero jacket with gold trim. Her black crinoline skirt flared out just above her knee. Her spiky leather boots would be killing her feet by now, but the look was worth it.

"Mascara?" Nancy asked.

Julia studied the skin around her eyes, looking for smears. "Nope. Me?"

"Mahhvelous," she drawled a perfect Billy Crystal.

The line finally moved, and Julia went into the first stall. She felt her pager vibrate as she started to unbutton her jeans. She didn't scroll the number right away. She sat down on the toilet. She looked up at the ceiling. She looked at the posters taped to the back of the stall door. She finally looked down at the pager. She pressed the button to scroll the number.

222.

Her heart broke into a million pieces.

222.

Julia looked up, trying to keep her tears from falling. She sniffed. She counted to a slow one hundred. She looked down again, because maybe she was wrong.

222.

Robin couldn't get away from his parents.

Or maybe he could get away, but he didn't want to. Maybe Julia had been awful this afternoon. Maybe she was boring. Maybe Robin knew she hadn't orgasmed, or she had orgasmed too loudly or breathed too hard or sounded too silly or—

"God!" somebody groaned.

Julia heard the distinctive sound of vomit hitting toilet water. It had to be Alabama, aka Deanie Crowder. The sound of her retching was like a duck being sucked through a tuba.

Nancy dry heaved. She had been a sympathetic vomiter since an ill-fated Pilgrim's feast in kindergarten. Julia heard her stiletto boots snapping against the concrete as she rushed out of the bathroom.

Instead of going after her, Julia leaned back against the toilet tank. She held the pager in her hand, praying it would vibrate again, that she would press the button and see 111—*Yes, I can get away, please meet me at my parents' house because I love you.*

Robin hadn't actually said that he loved her. Was she

a fool for being with him like that when he hadn't even told her that above everyone else, it was Julia who had his heart?

Someone banged on the stall door. "Ladies gotta pee out here!"

Julia flushed the toilet. She stood up. She pushed open the door. She washed her hands. She went back to the bar and stood close enough to Top Gun for him to get the message.

"Buy you a drink?" Up close, he was more of a Goose, but Julia was past caring about that kind of thing.

She smiled sweetly. "I love those Moscow Mules." She didn't actually, but the vodka, ginger ale, and lime cocktail cost $4.50 and was a more expedient way to get drunk than the dollar PBRs they drank when they had to pick up their own tabs.

"I like the way you dance," Top Gun told her.

Julia threw back the drink. "Let's go."

He followed her onto the dance floor, where he proved to be an even worse dancer than Julia. He shuffled side to side. He kept his elbows bent, his fingers snapping. Sometimes he looked down and over his shoulder, an approximation of a man making sure he hadn't stepped in dog shit.

At least Julia put her heart into it, throwing out her arms, wiggling her hips when C+C Music Factory told everybody to dance now. Top Gun dropped away when Lisa Lisa came on. "Head to Toe." Julia closed her eyes and tried not to think about Robin. She didn't know if he liked dancing. Maybe he didn't even like Madonna.

Maybe he'd just said that to get into her pants. Or maybe he'd said it because he really loved her. Why would he talk about having a son, working at his father's bakery, if he wasn't thinking about his future?

Or maybe he was thinking about his future without her.

Julia couldn't be around all these people anymore. The crush of the dance floor was too much. She pushed her way through the crowd. She found her purse hooked on the bar stool where she'd left it. She rummaged past her toothbrush and hairbrush and toiletries and change of underwear that she'd packed in anticipation of not going back to her dorm that night. Her lip gloss felt cold on her lips, because she was sweating and it was hot in the bar. Some older guy had bought her a second Moscow Mule. The ice had melted. The liquid had turned from gold to tan. She drank it anyway. The vodka hit the back of her throat like a hammer.

"Whoa there." Nancy patted her back until Julia stopped coughing. "You okay?"

"What time is it?"

Nancy checked Julia's watch. "It's exactly ten thirty-eight in the evening."

She'd been dancing for less than an hour. It had felt like an eternity. "I wanna go back."

"Why don't you wait until eleven and we'll go together?"

"No, my head is killing me." Julia put her hand to her head, which actually did hurt.

Nancy said, "You were the one who said we shouldn't go out alone."

"Only if we're drunk, and I'm not drunk." Actually, Julia felt a bit light-headed, but that was probably because her broken heart was sitting at the bottom of her stomach. "Thanks for coming out tonight. It really meant a lot. I'm sorry Michael Stipe didn't show up."

"I didn't really think he would." Nancy looked at her like she was acting weird. Maybe she was. "Sure you're okay?"

Julia said, "I love you, buddy. You're a good friend."

"Aw." Nancy rubbed her back again. "I love you, too, buddy."

Julia unhooked her purse from the back of the chair. The floor was still crowded with dancers and lingerers and students who would regret their indulgences when their alarms went off in the morning. Thank God Julia didn't have any classes tomorrow. She would go home to her room in the Boulevard house and sulk around in her pajamas and cuddle all the cats and dogs around her and watch soap operas all day.

She pushed open the heavy metal door. The night air was the most welcome feeling that Julia had ever experienced. With every step, she felt her lungs open up like petals on a flower. Her head spun from all the fresh oxygen. She held out her arms as she walked down the empty sidewalk, embracing the night, embracing the clarity it brought.

As her grandmother might say, Julia needed to get ahold of herself.

Robin Clark was sweet and kind and gentle and wonderful and she loved being with him and might even be in love with him, but he was not the sole reason her world turned on its axis.

Julia was nineteen years old. She was going to write her first front-page story. She was going to graduate at the top of her class from one of the best journalism schools in the country. She had good health. She had good friends. She had a loving family. Instead of being some silly teenager whose heart rose and fell depending on how a boy felt (or might feel) about her, she needed to act like a grown woman and look at the facts. Robin had called her pager to tell her that he couldn't come. If he was writing Julia off, if he had just used her for sex, then he wouldn't bother to sneak to the ranger's station and risk his family's wrath.

Right?

Because Julia knew that Robin's father took this camping thing very seriously. It was an annual affair. He closed down the bakery the first week of every March. He took his entire family into the woods so he could spend time with them. And Robin was honoring that. He was a good guy. He was like Julia's father, and Mr. Hannah, and David Conford, and her Grandpa Ernie. He wasn't like Greg or Lionel or Professor Edwards, who was probably at this very moment telling one of his unsuspecting students that he'd love to talk to her more about her paper over coffee and did she know that his apartment was just across campus.

The poor girl. She was probably a freshman. Young.

Naïve. Greg had said that Jenny Loudermilk was a freshman. At least she was until she dropped out of school. She was walking down Broad Street and in a second, her whole life had changed. She would never again be that girl who walked around without a care in the world.

Twenty-two women in Athens would have their lives changed like that this year. And next year. And the year after. Not to mention the ones who had it happen before.

It was some kind of horrible that your odds got better every time another woman was raped. Assaulted. Attacked. Threatened. Like the clock in Times Square counting down the ball every New Years' Eve.

Beatrice Oliver: #22.

Jenny Loudermilk: #21.

Mona No-Name: #20.

Who would be #19? Some sloppy drunk freshman? The girl who was having coffee with Professor Edwards across town? Deanie Crowder, who had puked out her guts in the bathroom at the bar? Nancy would walk her home. Somebody should walk her home.

Julia stumbled over a broken bit of sidewalk. Suddenly, she felt very dizzy. Her stomach roiled. The drink. Maybe the vodka was bad. Or the ginger ale, though she wasn't sure that bad soda was anything but flat. It couldn't make you sick, but she felt sick. She braced herself against the wall and felt a stream of hot liquid come out of her mouth.

Julia covered her face with her hands. Something was wrong. She tried to get her bearings. Her parents were at

Harry Bissett's, just a few blocks away. They wouldn't be happy to see her like this, but they would be devastated if they found out she'd needed them and didn't reach out.

She cut through a side street. Her knees felt wobbly. She leaned against a smelly trash can. Stickers were plastered all over the side. Phish. Poison. Stryker. She tried to read the street sign. Her eyes synthesized the words into white blotches on green.

Her parents couldn't be far. She pushed away from the trash can. She tried to focus on the sidewalk ahead of her. Each step was an effort. She had to rest against an old Cadillac to catch her breath. She stared down at tailfins the size of surfboards. Her father loved the Beach Boys. They'd bought him *Still Cruisin'* for Christmas a few years ago. He was so much happier than when they gave him a book about being old for his last birthday.

"You look lost."

Julia spun around.

There was a black van parked in front of the Cadillac. The side door was open. A man was in the shadows. She knew him. She had seen his face before, maybe several times before. Today? Over the weekend? Downtown? On campus? The information was so close, but she couldn't get her mind to make the connection.

"I'm sorry," Julia said, because she always apologized for everything.

He got out of the van.

Julia stepped back, but the sidewalk had turned to sand.

He walked toward her.

"Please," she whispered. Her sisters. Her parents. Robin. Nancy. Deanie. Beatrice Oliver. Jenny Loudermilk. Mona No-Name.

In the end, he didn't wrap his hand around her mouth or put a knife to her throat.

He just punched her in the face.

Julia Carroll: #19.

AUTHOR'S NOTE: I phudged a bit on the Phish concert date (it was March 1) but it makes sense those guys would still be there, right? The numbers I quoted from the FBI's Uniform Crime Reporting Program (UCRP) are actually from 1991, the year during which this story is set. As of 2013, the term "forcible rape" was replaced with "rape," and the definition was changed to be more inclusive (statutory rape and incest data are still not included in this figure). The CDC estimates that upward to 80% of sexual assaults go unreported. According to the latest Crime Clock data, in America in 2013, a woman was raped every 6.6 minutes.

Coming from William Morrow
in September 2015

KARIN SLAUGHTER

PRETTY GIRLS

Her electrifying new novel

Prologue

WHEN YOU FIRST disappeared, your mother warned me that finding out exactly what had happened to you would be worse than never knowing. We argued about this constantly because arguing was the only thing that held us together at the time.

"Knowing the details won't make it any easier," she warned me. "The details will tear you apart."

I was a man of science. I needed facts. Whether I wanted to or not, my mind would not stop generating hypotheses: Abducted. Raped. Defiled.

Rebellious.

That was the sheriff's theory, or at least his excuse when we demanded answers he could not give. Your mother and I had always been secretly pleased that you were so headstrong and passionate about your causes. Once you were gone, we understood that these were the

qualities that painted young men as smart and ambitious
and young women as trouble.

"Girls run off all the time." The sheriff had shrugged
like you were any girl, like a week would pass—a month,
maybe a year—and you would come back into our lives
offering a half-hearted apology about a boy you'd followed or a friend you'd joined on a trip across the ocean.

You were nineteen years old. Legally, you did not
belong to us anymore. You belonged to yourself. You belonged to the world.

Still, we organized search parties. We kept calling
hospitals and police stations and homeless shelters. We
posted fliers around town. We knocked on doors. We
talked to your friends. We checked abandoned buildings
and burned-out houses on the bad side of town. We hired
a private detective who took half of our savings and a psy-
chic who took most of the rest. We appealed to the media,
though the media lost interest when there were no sala-
cious details to breathlessly report.

This is what we knew: You were in a bar. You didn't
drink any more than usual. You told your friends that
you weren't feeling well and that you were going to walk
home and that was the last time anyone ever reported
seeing you.

Over the years, there were many false confessions.
Sadists rallied around the mystery of where you'd gone.
They provided details that could not be proven, leads that
could not be followed. At least they were honest when
they were caught out. The psychics always blamed me for
not looking hard enough.

Because I never stopped looking.

I understand why your mother gave up. Or at least had to appear to. She had to rebuild a life—if not for herself, for what was left of her family. Your little sister was still at home. She was quiet and furtive and hanging out with the kind of girls who would talk her into doing things she should not do. Like sneak into a bar to hear music and never come home again.

On the day we signed our divorce papers, your mother told me that her only hope was that one day we would find your body. That was what she clung to, the idea that one day, eventually, we could lay you down in your final resting place.

I said that we might just find you in Chicago or Santa Fe or Portland or some artistic commune that you had wandered off to because you were always a free spirit.

Your mother was not surprised to hear me say this. This was a time when the pendulum of hope still swung back and forth between us, so that some days she took to her bed with sorrow and some days she came home from the store with a shirt or a sweater or a pair of jeans that she would give you when you returned home to us.

I remember clearly the day I lost my hope. I was working at the veterinary office downtown. Someone brought in an abandoned dog. The creature was pitiful, obviously abused. He was mostly yellow Lab, though his fur was ashen from the elements. Barbs were clumped in his haunches. There were hot spots on his bare skin where he'd scratched too much or licked too much or done the things dogs try to do when they are left alone to soothe themselves.

I spent some time with him to let him know he was safe. I let him lick the back of my hand. I let him get used to my scent. After he calmed, I started the examination. He was an older dog, but until recently, his teeth had been well kept. A surgical scar indicated that at some point, an injured knee had been carefully and expensively repaired. The obvious abuse the animal suffered had not yet worked its way into his muscle memory. Whenever I put my hand to his face, the weight of his head fell into the palm of my hand.

I looked into the dog's woeful eyes and my mind filled in details from this poor creature's life. I had no way of knowing the truth, but my heart understood this was what had happened: He had not been abandoned. He had wandered off or slipped his leash. His owners had gone to the store or left for vacation and somehow—a gate accidentally left open, a fence jumped, a door left ajar by a well-meaning house sitter—this beloved creature had found himself walking the streets with no sense of which direction would take him back home.

And a group of kids or an unspeakable monster or a combination of all had found this dog and turned him from a cherished pet into a hunted animal.

Like my father, I have devoted my life to treating animals, but that was the first time I had ever made the connection between the horrible things people do to animals and the even more horrific things they do to other human beings.

Here was how a chain ripped flesh. Here was the damage wrought by kicking feet and punching fists. Here is what a human being looked like when they wandered off into a world that did not cherish them, did not love them, did not ever want them to go home.

Your mother was right.

The details tore me apart.

Chapter One

THE DOWNTOWN ATLANTA restaurant was empty except for a lone businessman in a corner booth and a bartender who seemed to think he had mastered the art of flirty conversation. The pre-dinner rush was starting its slow wind-up. Cutlery and china clashed in the kitchen. The chef bellowed. A waiter huffed a laugh. The television over the bar offered a low, steady beat of bad news.

Claire Scott tried to ignore the endless drum of noise as she sat at the bar nursing her second club soda. Paul was ten minutes late. He was never late. He was usually ten minutes early. It was one of the things she teased him about but really needed him to do.

"Another?"

"Sure." Claire smiled politely at the bartender. He had been trying to engage her from the moment she sat down. He was young and handsome, which should've been flattering but just made her feel old—not because she was ancient, but because she had noticed that the closer she got to forty, the more annoyed she was by people in their twenties. They were constantly making her think of sentences that began with "when I was your age."

"Third one." His voice took on a teasing tone as he refilled her glass of club soda. "You're hittin' 'em pretty hard."

"Am I?"

He winked at her. "You let me know if you need a ride home."

Claire laughed because it was easier than telling him to brush his hair out of his eyes and go back to college. She checked the time on her phone again. Paul was now twelve minutes late. She started catastrophizing: carjacking, hit by a bus, struck by a falling piece of airplane fuselage, abducted by a madman.

The front door opened, but it was a group of people, not Paul. They were all dressed in business casual, likely workers from the surrounding office buildings who wanted to grab an early drink before heading home to the suburbs and their parents' basements.

"You been following this?" The bartender nodded toward the television.

"Not really," Claire said, though of course she'd been following the story. You couldn't turn on the TV without hearing about the missing teenage girl. Sixteen years old. White. Middle class. Very pretty. No one ever seemed quite as outraged when an ugly woman went missing.

"Tragic," he said. "She's so beautiful."

Claire looked at her phone again. Paul was now thirteen minutes late. Today of all days. He was an architect, not a brain surgeon. There was no emergency so dire that he couldn't take two seconds to text or give her a call.

She started spinning her wedding ring around her finger, which was a nervous habit she didn't know she had until Paul had pointed it out to her. They had been arguing about something that had seemed desperately important to Claire at the time but now she couldn't remember the topic or even when the argument had occurred. Last week? Last month? She had known Paul for eighteen years, been married to him for almost as long. There wasn't much left that they could argue about with any conviction.

"Sure I can't interest you in something harder?" The bartender was holding up a bottle of Stoli, but his meaning was clear.

Claire forced another laugh. She had known this type of man her entire life. Tall, dark and handsome with twinkling eyes and a mouth that moved like honey. At twelve, she would've scribbled his name all over her math notebook. At sixteen, she would've let him put his hand up her sweater. At twenty, she would've let him put his hand up anything he wanted. And now, at thirty-eight, she just wanted him to go away.

She said, "No thank you. My parole officer has advised me not to drink unless I'm going to be home all evening."

He gave her a smile that said he didn't quite get the joke. "Bad girl. I like it."

"You should've seen me in my ankle monitor." She winked at him. "Black is the new orange."

The front door opened. Paul. Claire felt a wave of relief as he walked toward her.

She said, "You're late."

Paul kissed her cheek. "Sorry. No excuse. I should've called. Or texted."

"Yes, you should've."

He told the bartender, "Glenfiddich; single, neat."

Claire watched the young man pour Paul's Scotch with a previously unseen professionalism. Her wedding ring, her gentle brush-offs and her outright rejection had been minor obstacles compared to the big no of another man kissing her cheek.

"Sir." He placed the drink in front of Paul, then headed toward the other end of the bar.

Claire lowered her voice. "He offered me a ride home."

Paul looked at the man for the first time since he'd walked through the door. "Should I go punch him in the nose?"

"Yes."

"Will you take me to the hospital when he punches me back?"

"Yes."

Paul smiled, but only because she was smiling, too. "So, how does it feel to be untethered?"

Claire looked down at her naked ankle, half expecting to see a bruise or mark where the chunky black ankle bracelet had been. Six months had passed since she'd worn a skirt in public, the same amount of time she'd been wearing the court-ordered monitoring device. "It feels like freedom."

He straightened the straw by her drink, making it parallel to the napkin. "You're constantly tracked with your phone and the GPS in your car."

"I can't be sent to jail every time I put down my phone or leave my car."

Paul shrugged off the point, which she thought was a very good one. "What about curfew?"

"It's lifted. As long as I stay out of trouble for the next year, my record will be expunged and it'll be like it never even happened."

"Magic."

"More like a very expensive lawyer."

He grinned. "It's cheaper than that bracelet you wanted from Cartier."

"Not if you add in the earrings." They shouldn't joke about this, but the alternative was to take it very seriously. She said, "It's weird. I know the monitor's not there anymore, but I can still feel it."

"Signal detection theory." He straightened the straw again. "Your perceptual systems are biased toward the monitor touching your skin. More often, people experience the sensation with their phones. They feel it vibrating even when it's not."

That's what she got for marrying a geek.

Paul stared at the television. "You think they'll find her?"

Claire didn't respond. She looked down at the drink in Paul's hand. She'd never liked the taste of Scotch, but being told she shouldn't drink had made her want to go on a week-long bender.

This afternoon, out of desperation for something to

say, Claire had told her court-appointed psychiatrist that she absolutely despised being told what to do. "Who the hell doesn't?" the blowsy woman had demanded, slightly incredulous. Claire had felt her cheeks turn red, but she knew better than to say that she was particularly bad about it, that she had landed herself in court-appointed therapy for that very reason. She wasn't going to give the woman the satisfaction of a breakthrough.

Besides, Claire had come to that realization on her own the minute the handcuffs were clamped around her wrists.

"Idiot," she had mumbled to herself as the cop had guided her into the back of the squad car.

"That's going in my report," the woman had briskly informed her.

They were all women that day, female police officers of varying sizes and shapes with thick leather belts around their chunky waists carrying all manner of lethal devices. Claire felt that things would've gone a lot better if at least one of them had been a man, but sadly, that was not the case. This is where feminism had gotten her: locked in the back of a sticky squad car with the skirt on her tennis dress riding up her thighs.

At the jail, Claire's wedding ring, watch, and tennis shoelaces had been taken by a large woman with a mole between her hairy eyebrows whose general appearance reminded Claire of a stink bug. There was no hair growing out of the mole, and Claire wanted to ask why she bothered to pluck the mole but not her eyebrows but it was too late because another woman, this one tall and reedy like a praying mantis, was already taking Claire into the next room.

The fingerprinting was nothing like on TV. Instead of ink, Claire had to press her fingers onto a filthy glass plate so the swirls could be digitized into a computer. Her swirls, apparently, were very faint. It took several tries.

"Good thing I didn't rob a bank," Claire said, then added, "ha ha," to convey the humor.

"Press evenly," the praying mantis said, chewing off the wings of a fly.

Claire's mugshot was taken against a white background with a ruler that was clearly off by an inch. She wondered aloud why she wasn't asked to hold a sign with her name and inmate number.

"Photoshop template," the praying mantis said in a bored tone that indicated the question was not a new one.

It was the only picture Claire had ever taken where no one had told her to smile.

Then a third policewoman who, bucking the trend, had a nose like a mallard, had taken Claire to the holding cell where, surprisingly, Claire was not the only woman in a tennis outfit.

"What're you in for?" the other tennis-outfitted inmate had asked. She looked hard and strung out and had obviously been arrested while playing with a different set of balls.

"Murder," Claire had said, because she had already decided that she wasn't going to take this seriously.

"Hey." Paul had finished his Scotch and was signaling

the bartender for a refill. "What are you thinking about over there?"

She let out a long sigh. "I'm thinking your day was probably worse than mine if you're ordering a second drink." Paul rarely drank. It was something they had in common. Neither one of them liked feeling out of control, which had made jail a real bummer, ha ha.

She asked him, "Everything all right?"

"It's good right now." He rubbed her back with his hand. "What did the shrink say?"

Claire waited until the bartender had returned to his corner. "She said that I'm not being forthcoming about my emotions."

"That's not like you at all."

They smiled at each other. Another old argument that wasn't worth having anymore.

"I don't like being analyzed," Claire said, and she could picture her analyst offering an exaggerated shrug as she demanded, "Who the hell does?"

"You know what I was thinking today?" Paul took her hand. His palm felt rough. He'd been working in the garage all weekend. "I was thinking about how much I love you."

"That's a funny thing for a husband to say to his wife."

"It's true, though." Paul pressed her hand to his lips. "I can't imagine what my life would be like without you."

"Tidier," she said, because Paul was the one who was always picking up abandoned shoes and various items of clothing that should've been put in the laundry basket but somehow ended up in front of the bathroom sink.

He said, "I know things are hard right now. Especially with—" He tilted his head toward the television, which was showing a new photo of the missing sixteen-year-old.

Claire looked at the set. The girl really was beautiful. Athletic and lean with dark, wavy hair.

Paul said, "I just want you to know that I'm always going to be here for you. No matter what."

Claire felt her throat start to tighten. She took him for granted sometimes. That was the luxury of a long marriage. But she knew that she loved him. She needed him. He was the anchor that kept her from drifting away.

He said, "You know that you're the only woman I've ever loved."

She invoked her college predecessor. "Ava Guilford would be shocked to hear that."

"Don't play. I'm being serious." He leaned in so close that his forehead almost touched hers. "You are the love of my life, Claire Scott. You're everything to me."

"Despite my criminal record?"

He kissed her. Really kissed her. She tasted Scotch and a hint of peppermint and felt a rush of pleasure when his fingers stroked the inside of her thigh.

When they stopped for air, she said, "Let's go home."

Paul finished his drink in one swallow. He tossed some cash onto the bar. His hand stayed at Claire's back as they left the restaurant. A cold gust of wind picked at the hem of her skirt. Paul rubbed her arm to keep her warm. He was walking so close to her that she could feel his breath on her neck. "Where are you parked?"

"Parking deck," she said.

"I'm on the street." He handed his keys to her. "Take my car."

"Let's go together."

"Let's go here." He pulled her into an alley and pressed her back against the wall.

Claire opened her mouth to ask what had gotten into him, but then he was kissing her. His hand slid underneath her skirt. Claire gasped, but not so much because he took her breath away as because the alley was not dark and the street was not empty. She could see men in suits strolling by, heads turning, eyes tracking the scene until the last moment. This was how people ended up on the Internet.

"Paul." She put her hand to his chest, wondering what had happened to her vanilla husband who thought it was kinky if they did it in the guest room. "People are watching."

"Back here." He took her hand, leading her deeper into the alley.

Claire stepped over a graveyard of cigarette butts as she followed him. The alley was T-shaped, intersecting with another service alley for the restaurants and shops. Hardly a better situation. She imagined fry cooks standing at open doors with cigarettes in their mouths and iPhones in their hands. Even without spectators, there were all kinds of reasons she should not do this.

Then again, no one liked being told what to do.

Paul pulled her around a corner. Claire had a quick moment to scan their empty surroundings before her back was pressed against another wall. His mouth covered hers.

His hands cupped her ass. He wanted this so badly that she started to want it, too. She closed her eyes and let herself give in. Their kisses deepened. He tugged down her underwear. She helped him, shuddering because it was cold and it was dangerous and she was so ready that she didn't care anymore.

"Claire . . ." he whispered in her ear. "Tell me you want this."

"I want this."

"Tell me again."

"I want this."

Without warning, he spun her around. Claire's cheek grazed the brick. He had her pinned to the wall. She pushed back against him. He groaned, taking the move for excitement, but she could barely breathe.

"Paul—"

"Don't move."

Claire understood the words, but her brain took several seconds to process the fact that they had not come from her husband's mouth.

"Turn around."

Paul started to turn.

"Not you, asshole."

Her. He meant her. Claire couldn't move. Her legs were shaking. She could barely hold herself up.

"I said turn the fuck around."

Paul's hands gently wrapped around Claire's arms. She stumbled as he slowly turned her around.

There was a man standing directly behind Paul. He was wearing a black hoodie zipped just below his thick, tattooed neck. A sinister-looking rattlesnake arced across his Adam's apple, its fangs showing in a wicked grin.

"Hands up." The snake's mouth bobbed as the man spoke.

"We don't want trouble." Paul's hands were in the air. His body was perfectly still. Claire looked at him. He nodded once, telling her it was going to be okay when clearly it was not. "My wallet's in my back pocket."

The man wrenched out the wallet with one hand. Claire could only assume a gun was in the other. She saw it in her mind's eye: black and shiny, pressed into Paul's back.

"Here." Paul took off his wedding ring, his class ring, his watch. Patek Philippe. She had bought it for him five years ago. His initials were on the back.

"Claire," Paul's voice was strained, "give him your wallet."

Claire stared at her husband. She felt the insistent tapping of her carotid artery pulsing in her neck. Paul had a gun at his back. They were being robbed. That's what was going on. This was real. This was happening. She looked down at her hand, the movement tracking slowly because she was in shock and terrified and didn't know what to do. Her fingers were still wrapped around Paul's keys. She'd been holding onto them the entire time. How could she have sex with him if she was still holding his keys?

"Claire," Paul repeated, "get your wallet."

She dropped the keys into her purse. She pulled out her wallet and handed it to the man.

He jammed it into his pocket, then held out his hand again. "Phone."

Claire retrieved her iPhone. All of her contacts. Her vacation photos from the last few years. St. Martin. London. Paris. Munich.

"The ring, too." The man glanced up and down the alley. Claire did the same. There was no one. Even the side streets were empty. Her back was still to the wall. The corner leading to the main road was an arm's length away. There were people on the street. Lots of people.

The man read her thoughts. "Don't be stupid. Take off the ring."

Claire took off her wedding ring. This was okay to lose. They had insurance. It wasn't even her original ring. They had picked it out years ago when Paul had finally finished his internship and passed his Registration Exam.

"Earrings," the man ordered. "Come on, bitch, move."

Claire reached up to her earlobe. Her hands had started to tremble. She hadn't remembered putting in the diamond studs this morning, but now she could see herself standing in front of her jewelry box.

Was this her life passing before her eyes—vacant recollections of *things*?

"Hurry." The man waved his free hand to urge her on.

Claire fumbled with the backs on the diamond studs. A tremble made her fingers thick and useless. She saw herself at Tiffany picking out the earrings. Thirty-second birthday. Paul giving her a "can you believe we're doing this?" look as the saleslady took them back to the special secret room where high-dollar purchases were made.

Claire dropped the earrings in the man's open hand. She was shaking. Her heart beat like a snare drum.

"That's it." Paul turned around. His back was pressed against Claire. Blocking her. Protecting her. He still had his hands in the air. "You have everything."

Claire could see the man over Paul's shoulder. He wasn't holding a gun. He was holding a knife. A long, sharp knife with a serrated edge and a hook at the point that looked like the sort of thing a hunter would use to gut an animal.

Paul said, "There's nothing else. Just go."

The man didn't go. He was looking at Claire like he'd found something more expensive to steal than her thirty-six-thousand-dollar earrings. His lips tweaked in a smile. One of his front teeth was plated in gold. She realized that the rattlesnake tattoo had a matching gold fang.

And then she realized that this wasn't just a robbery.

So did Paul. He said, "I have money."

"No shit." The man's fist hammered into Paul's chest. Claire felt the impact in her own chest, his shoulder blades cutting into her collarbone. His head snapping into her face. The back of her head banged against the brick wall.

Claire was momentarily stunned. Stars fireworked in front of her eyes. She tasted blood in her mouth. She blinked. She looked down. Paul was writhing on the ground.

"Paul—" She reached for him but her scalp ignited in white-hot pain. The man had grabbed her by the hair. He wrenched her down the alley. Claire stumbled. Her knee grazed the pavement. The man kept walking, almost jogging. She had to bend at the waist to alleviate some of the agony. One of her heels broke off. She tried to look back. Paul was clutching his arm like he was having a heart attack.

"No," she whispered, even as she wondered why she wasn't screaming. "No-no-no."

The man dragged her forward. Claire could hear herself wheezing. Her lungs had filled with sand. He was taking her toward the side street. There was a black van that she hadn't noticed before. Claire dug her fingernails into his wrist. He jerked her head. She tripped. He jerked her again. The pain was excruciating, but it was nothing compared to the terror. She wanted to scream. She needed to scream. But her throat was choked closed by the knowledge of what was coming. He was going to take her somewhere else in that van. Somewhere private. Somewhere awful that she might not ever leave again.

"No . . ." she begged. "Please . . . no . . . no . . ."

The man let go of Claire, but not because she'd asked him to. He spun around, the knife out in front of him. Paul was up on his feet. He was running toward the man. He let out a guttural howl as he lunged into the air.

It all happened very quickly. Too quickly. There was no slowing of time so that Claire could bear witness to every millisecond of her husband's struggle.

Paul could've outrun this man on a treadmill or solved an equation before the guy had a chance to sharpen his pencil, but his opponent had something over Paul Scott that they didn't teach in graduate school: how to fight with a knife.

There was only a whistling noise as the blade sliced

through the air. Claire had expected more sounds: a sudden slap as the hooked tip of the knife punctured Paul's skin. A grinding noise as the serrated edge sawed past his ribs. A scrape as the blade separated tendon and cartilage.

Paul's hands went to his belly. The pearl handle of the knife stuck up between his fingers. He stumbled back against the wall, mouth open, eyes almost comically wide. He was wearing his navy blue Tom Ford suit that was too tight across his shoulders. Claire had made a mental note to get the seam let out but now it was too late because the jacket was soaked with blood.

Paul looked down at his hands. The blade was sunk in to the hilt, almost equidistant between his navel and his heart. His blue shirt flowered with blood. He looked shocked. They were both shocked. They were supposed to have an early dinner tonight, celebrate Claire's successful navigation of the criminal justice system, not bleed to death in a cold, dank alley.

She heard footsteps. The Snake Man was running away, their rings and jewelry jangling in his pockets.

"Help," Claire said, but it was a whisper, so low that she could barely hear the sound of her own voice. "H-help," she stuttered. But who could help them? Paul was always the one who brought help. Paul was the one who took care of everything.

Until now.

He slid down the brick wall and landed hard on the ground. Claire knelt beside him. Her hands moved out in front of her but she didn't know where to touch him.

Eighteen years of loving him. Eighteen years of sharing his bed. She had pressed her hand to his forehead to check for fevers, wiped his face when he was sick, kissed his lips, his cheeks, his eyelids, even slapped him once out of anger, but now she did not know where to touch him.

"Claire."

Paul's voice. She knew his voice. Claire went to her husband. She wrapped her arms and legs around him. She pulled him close to her chest. She pressed her lips to the side of his head. She could feel the heat leaving his body. "Paul, please. Be okay. You have to be okay."

"I'm okay," Paul said, and it seemed like the truth until it wasn't anymore. The tremor started in his legs and worked into a violent shaking by the time it reached the rest of his body. His teeth chattered. His eyelids fluttered.

He said, "I love you."

"Please," she whispered, burying her face in his neck. She smelled his aftershave. Felt a rough patch of beard he'd missed with the razor this morning. Everywhere she touched him, his skin was so very, very cold. "Please don't leave me, Paul. Please."

"I won't," he promised.

But then he did.

About the Author

Karin Slaughter is the #1 internationally bestselling author of more than a dozen novels, including the Will Trent and Grant County series and the instant *New York Times* bestseller *Cop Town*. There are more than 30 million copies of her books in print around the world.

Her new novel *Pretty Girls* will be published in September 2015.

www.karinslaughter.com

Discover great authors, exclusive offers, and more at hc.com.